indebted

A Kingpin Love Affair Vol: 1

J. L. Beck

Cover design by Sprinkles on Top Studio LLC
Cover and interior photos by Shutterstock
Editing by Tina Donaldson
Formatting by That Formatting Lady (Angela Shockley)

Copyright 2014 by Josi Beck
All rights reserved.

More by J.L. Beck

The Bittersweet Series:
(New Adult Contemporary)

BITTERSWEET REVENGE
BITTERSWEET LOVE
BITTERSWEET HATE
BITTERSWEET SYMPHONY
BITTERSWEET TRUST

A Kingpin Love Affair:
(Dark Romance)
INDEBTED (Vol: 1)

This book is intended for readers 18+ only. It is a dark, erotic romance that contains copious amounts of violence, sex, murder, swearing, dubious content, and other things that aren't suitable for anyone but adults. This book also contains graphic abuse, some that may trigger unwanted or hidden emotions.

Please be advised that I do NOT condone this type of behavior, and I do NOT agree with emotional and/or physical abuse in any way, shape, or form. This is a work of fiction, and nothing contained in it is based off of my life or someone else's life experiences. Please heed the warning when I say that this is dark. It is not rainbow and ponies; it is murder, and darkness that blooms into love.

Dedication

To Brie, my friend and personal assistant: Without you, this book never would have come about. Thank you for all you do and for the love you share in my books. I love you like tan leggings!!!

table of contents

Past: Zerro

"Momma!" I cried out. My body shook with every breath. I couldn't find her even though I heard her scream. I had never heard my mother scream like that before. My stomach twisted in knots as fear coursed through me. Maybe the maid had just snuck up on her?

I circled down the stairs and down the hall to her room. I was just outside her door when I heard her scream again. It wasn't the scream that she made when she was scared; it was a different scream, a terrifying scream.

"Just take me! Leave Alzerro alone!" I heard my mother cry. I wanted to run to her, to hold and protect her. Something was holding me in place, though. I knew if whoever had my momma saw I was there, they would take me.

"The boy will be a mafia king someday. Did you think we would just leave him here with you?" It sounded as if this man was screaming at her, but his voice wasn't raised. The hairs on the back of my neck stood on end as I continued to listen to her pleas. Where were the bodyguards? Why were they not saving her?

"The boy is ours," the man I hadn't seen yet said. Then I heard it, the last cry, the last plea leaving my mother's lips. A gunshot went off, the sound reverberating through me. One shot that forever changed my life by taking away the only person I loved, the only person who loved me. I prayed my mother hadn't been shot, but I knew she had been.

"Remove her body from the house. I don't want the boy finding it." I turned on my heels as the man's voice grew closer to the door. Everything in me said I needed to run, to hide. I couldn't let him see me, nor did I want to see him.

I ran up the stairs with all my might to my room where I shut the door and locked it. I knew it would do no good if they had guns, but I had to try. Whoever they were, they were bad men.

Not even a minute later, the door handle shook. My body quaked in fear as I took as many steps away from it as I could.

I heard the wood splintering against the weight of whoever was on the other side. I knew I was quickly running out of time, but as I frantically looked around the room, I couldn't think of a place to hide.

Then my eyes landed on the closet. I scurried across the floor, my socks causing me to slide and fall. I had just closed my closet door when the door to my room came crashing down. Fear was rooted deep within my body, making it impossible for me to move. Why had these people killed my mother? What were they going to do to me?

Two men, covered in black from head to toe, stormed into my room. Their bodies were bigger than anyone I had ever seen. I wanted to be strong like my father always told me to be, but I couldn't be. I didn't want them to find me.

"Where is he?" one man said in frustration as he whipped the mattress from my bed. I watched from a slit in the closed door as they ripped my room to shreds. As they came closer to the door, I pushed further back into the closet until I came to the wall.

I knew I had to figure something out; my life depended on it. I felt along the wall to see if there were any hidden passages. I remembered all the times my mother and I played hide and seek. I was always trying to find the best hiding spots; my momma always pretended she couldn't find me. One of the times she "couldn't find me" while I was hiding in here, I watched her open a hidden wall. I never asked her about it, and she never mentioned the secret spot. It was as if she knew I would need it someday. I anxiously searched the wall until I found the distinct little wood piece that fit into the wall perfectly.

Pulling it out quietly, I crawled into the unknown space. It was a very small area, but I managed to sit down. The men's footsteps grew closer with every passing second, so I clumsily and quickly picked up the wood piece knowing if I made a mistake, I would be found.

My hands were sweating and shaking, and I felt like puking. I wanted to run to my mom; I wanted to be enveloped in the safety of her loving arms. I knew I would never feel her warmth again, though, and that broke my heart. However, I couldn't think about that because I needed to focus on hiding.

Just as I slid the wood into place, I heard the bad men enter the closet. The door flew open and hit the wall with a fierceness that shook me to my core. I heard them rip down my clothes that were on hangers and throw my boxes of prized possessions across the room.

"He's not fucking here," one of them growled. I listened to them shuffle around in my room as I forced my breaths to slow down. The darkness surrounded me, banishing all the light that I had in my life.

How could these people come into my house and kill my wonderful, kind, sweet mother? What did they want from me? How did they get in here? Who else did they kill? We had security, didn't we? Where were the maids? Were the bad people still here? Why did they leave me all alone?

As the house settled and the events filtered through my mind, I continued to sit in the small crawl space in the dark. I was terrified to come out and discover that my life really had been ripped away.

I didn't know how long I sat in the darkness, but at some point, a steely resolve settled in my heart and soul as I made a promise to my mother. Someday, when I was much older, I would make those bad men pay. I would find them and hurt them like they hurt my mother. They owed me their lives, and I would make sure they paid their debt.

Present (Seventeen Years Later): Zerro

I watched him slither in his seat. He was nervous; I could smell it without even seeing it. His eyes watched me carefully, trying to figure out what I would do next.

"Do you realize that borrowing money from the mafia, without the intent of paying it back, is the same as saying come and get me, I'm ready to die?" I kept my voice calm and cool. I could mean business without showing it. That's how I worked.

"We… I don't have any money, Zerro..." His voice was shakey and broken; he was so scared he could barely utter a word. I didn't care about his excuses for not having his payment. I only cared about him giving me my money, and that meant I had to do something to get it.

"Alzerro," I corrected him. I hated it when people who didn't know or care about me called me Zerro. My closest friends and family were the only ones allowed that privilege. When it came to business, you called me by my name. You would give me the respect I deserved, the respect I demanded.

"Alzerro," he quickly corrected himself. His chest was heaving, and sweat formed on his forehead. I could tell he thought he was going to die, and he would eventually, but I had something else in store for him first. I wanted my money back, and I would do whatever was necessary to get it. Whatever. Was. Necessary.

"I was afraid this would happen, so I went out of my way to dig up some dirt on you. Guess what I discovered? I found out you have a daughter. A very cute, young, naïve, innocent, intelligent daughter. I bet she's very capable of handling dear ol' Dad's debt, don't you think?" My voice was sinister, calm, and deadly. His face was a mask of confusion until what I said hit him square in the chest.

"No! Please! Bree has already suffered and lost so much. I borrowed the money for her to go off to college and lead a normal life… This is my debt to pay, not hers. Please, I beg of you. Please don't bring her into this." His features paled as his eyes brimmed with tears. He was at my mercy, yet his pleading meant nothing to me. I would love to say that I had a heart somewhere underneath my hatred, anger, and coldness, but I couldn't. I knew who I was, and I made no apologies for it.

"*I* didn't bring her into this, old man. *You* did," I hissed out, shoving his words back at him. He was trying to make me feel guilty, but situations like this never made me feel badly. If anything, it fueled the inferno inside of me and made me feel more powerful.

"Please…" he whispered as he began crying again. In that moment, all I could see were the tears that must have been falling from my mother's face when someone put a gun to her head and killed her. That man never even gave her the chance to beg or plead for her life. I prided myself on not being like that evil bastard; I, at least, was considerate enough to allow my debtors that chance before I killed them.

"You have two weeks until I come back to collect your debt. If you don't have it by then, I will be choosing your alternate payment. One way or another, you'll pay me." I smiled, simply because I was a sick bastard like that.

My men released him, and before I stepped out of the rundown farmhouse, my eyes landed on a photo of his daughter. She would be mine; she just didn't know it yet.

chapter one

Bree

It has been months since I've seen my dad. I had been really hesitant about leaving for college because I was leaving him all alone at the farm. I wasn't sure he could even make his own breakfast in the morning, do his laundry, or figure out how to run the vacuum. Mom had always catered to his needs, and after she died, I tried my best to take care of him and the house. He never asked or expected me to do most of the household chores like cooking, cleaning, and laundry, but I did them because I loved him. I pull my car onto our dirt road and instantly feel as if there's something wrong. I can't see the farmhouse yet, but that did nothing to ease the knots forming in my stomach.

Pulling around the bend and up into the driveway, I notice two black SUVs parked in front of the house. A man in a dark suit is standing outside of one, his hand on a shiny item at his hip.

Is that a gun? My mind is reeling as I try to figure out what the hell is going on. Is my dad okay? Why is this man at my house? Are there more men like him? There must be since there are two vehicles parked here. Are they robbing my house? Where is my dad?

I put my old Jeep into park and hesitate. Should I call 911? Isn't that what a rational person would do? Except from the way that this man is looking at me through the windshield, I get the feeling that calling 911 will do me no good.

Instead, I sit very still in the Jeep, wondering what his next move will be. His eyes roam over the house and then come back to my car. Time stands still for a few seconds before he comes walking toward the Jeep. My heart is beating out of my chest, and my eyes keep glancing down to my cellphone. I should call 911. What if these people are robbing us? What if they already killed my dad? I reach for my phone, knowing it might be my only chance…

"Get out of the car, and don't even fucking think about calling the cops," the man sternly instructs me through my open window. Damn it, I should have closed my window! His voice is loud and firm and sends shivers down my spine. There's a dark, evil look in his eyes that tells me he won't hesitate to shoot me if I try to run or be heroic.

"What is going on?" I demand. I don't want to be hurt or seen as weak, so I put on a brave face and try to act tough and unafraid. Before I can blink, the gun that was by his hip is pointed directly at my head. Oh shit. This guy means business. Serious, deadly business.

My breath catches in my chest. What the fuck is going on here? I come home from college and am staring down the barrel of a gun?

"Get out of the fucking car and don't ask questions," the man gruffly orders.

I shut my mouth immediately. I mean, a fucking gun is pointed at my face, so of course I'm going to do exactly as I'm told! For now, at least. I turn my Jeep off and slowly push the door open, hoping it will encourage him to ease off of me a little bit. However, it just makes him angrier.

With his free hand, the man yanks my door open as quickly as he can. For a moment, all I hear is the creaking from the rust build up.

I slip from the car with ease, my eyes never leaving him. What happens next is right out of a fucking movie. He grips the back of my head, pulling my hair. My scalp burns with his attack, and my eyes begin to fill with tears.

"Let go of me!" I demand, going loose in his hold. I won't allow whoever the fuck this person is to hurt me. His grip tightens, and I feel cold metal against my lips. My eyes grow as big as saucers the second I realize the barrel of the gun is against my lips, his finger on the trigger.

"Zerro has come to collect his debt." A sick smile crosses his face, and had I not been so incredibly terrified, I would've puked all over the ground. In that instant, I realize that whatever is about to happen isn't going to be good.

With the barrel still against my lips, I'm afraid to even ask what debt he's talking about. When Mom died, her life insurance policy left Dad and I enough money to get by. We weren't rich, but we weren't struggling either. Dad always told me our finances were fine. This man must have the wrong family, and he'll be sorry he treated me this way when he realizes the truth.

The gun slips over my bottom lip as lust and hunger fill his eyes.

"Zerro will have fun fucking every hole in your body. Then, when he's done with you and you're ready to be killed, I'll fuck you one last time…"

I sneer at him, anger building deep within me. Why does this man think he has a right to say such cruel, nasty, vile things to me? And who the hell is Zerro?

"I don't…" I begin to respond hotly.

"Shut your mouth!" he roars. His grip tightens as he pulls me up the steps to my home. The front door is kicked in, hanging on one hinge. Fear courses through me, making the anger I had been feeling just seconds ago disappear.

As we round the corner through the kitchen, my mouth almost falls open. I stare in disbelief at the scene in front of me: appliances ripped apart, cupboard doors hanging loosely on their hinges, food and other items strewn haphazardly around the usually immaculate room. It looks like a tornado has gone straight through the house! Pushing me forward, the man and I come to a halt just on the edge of entering the living room. My heart beats out of my chest when I hear my father's voice and see the puddle of blood on the floor.

Please tell me that isn't his blood. Please! I want to cry out, begging and pleading…

"I'm so sorry! I didn't have a choice, Bree!" my father chokes out when he sees me. There's a man holding him in place in one of the wooden dining room chairs. I want to cry as I take in his swollen face, the blood dripping from his lips, and the bruises that are already forming around his eyes and on his cheeks. His hands are tied securely behind his back, his wrists bleeding. I desperately want to go to him and comfort him, protect him from what is happening. My dad looks like he hasn't shaved, showered, or changed his clothes for quite some time. He seems to have stopped taking care of himself. The man sitting before me is just the shell of my father. The man before me is tired, worn out, broken, defeated, and hopeless. What the hell happened to my inspiring, courageous, easy-going, fun-loving dad? I was only gone for a few months! How could this have happened? Why didn't I know what was going on?

"Everyone has a choice, John," a deep, rich voice chides from somewhere. I look up as the man behind the mystery voice descends the stairs, his eyes landing on me.

There's an evil coldness in his stare that makes my heart skip a beat. His hair is dark and styled in a way that says he doesn't give two fucks about what anyone thinks. He wears a suit that looks like it cost more than the farmhouse. His chin is sharp and held high as if he believes he's above everyone else.

"I swear to you, Bree, I didn't have a choice. The bills were piling up: the mortgage, utilities, insurance, tuition… There just wasn't enough money for everything. The bank was going to foreclose on the farm, and your school was threatening to take action against you. The idea that you would have to drop out of your classes was killing me. I had to protect you and our home. I had no other choice." The words achingly and sorrowfully flow from him as shameful tears fill his eyes. It's difficult for any man to swallow his pride and admit he has problems.

I'm still not sure what is going on, though. I know we never had "extra" money to spend, but Dad always said it was okay. He told me that we always had enough to make ends meet. Anger surges through me as I realize he lied to me.

"You lied to me?" I question unbelievingly, though I'm certain I already know the answer. It's standing in my living room.

"Well, this is heartbreaking, but we should really consider getting down to business," the mystery man states unsympathetically. I have yet to learn the man's name, yet he has the audacity to sit on my father's sofa as if he owns the place.

"Who are you?" I ask bluntly. I'm not sure if I will get a straight answer as most, if not all, of the men in the room look like they work for the FBI.

"Who am I?" A smile quirks at the sides of his lips and laughter fills the room. My cheeks redden, and more anger finds its way into my already broken heart. As soon as his smile appears, though, it vanishes.

"I'm Alzerro King, sweetheart, and your dear ol' daddy owes me a lot of fucking money." My mouth drops open at his accusation.

"He doesn't," I deny vehemently. My father has already pretty much admitted to taking money from this man, but I still have to try to protect my dad. I have to find a way out of this mess. Why didn't he tell me he borrowed money from someone? The man who escorted me into my house pulls harder on my hair, causing me to grit my teeth tightly. I'm about five seconds from turning around and slapping this guy.

"See, that's where you're wrong. Your dad borrowed enough money to pay for a year's worth of school. Not only that, he paid the farm off and finished paying off the funeral costs." My eyes grow wide as tears threaten to leak from them. The secrets are accumulating at a rate that I can't even begin to believe.

My father went behind my back and borrowed money from someone dangerous. Why didn't he just go to a bank like other normal people? He lied and told me everything was okay. Looking at the big picture, it's clear to me that absolutely nothing is okay. Nothing about this situation is okay. Nothing about a gun being pointed at my father's head is okay!

"I was okay, Bree. Everything was okay until there was a bad storm, and we lost almost all of the crops. I couldn't afford to pay…" The earnestness in my father's voice tells me he's trying to make me understand. But how can I understand the lies and the danger we're now in?

"Shut the fuck up!" Alzerro yells, his words echoing off the drab walls of my country house. His voice is authoritative and commanding, as if his words hold a power that everyone bows to. He looks as if he's used to being obeyed and doesn't tolerate any insubordination. He looks right at me, his eyes possessing me. Their darkness is overwhelming and makes me wonder if any good can be found in him.

Silence falls over us as I push the tears away and put my thinking cap on. There has to be a way out of all of this. There has to be a way to earn the money back so we can pay these men back. The danger that surrounds these men tells me that it will be a mighty feat, but I'm not scared of a little hard work. My momma didn't raise no quitter.

My eyes scan the old, blue wallpaper that lines the living room walls. My mom had wanted it; in fact, she loved it so much that after we lost her to cancer, we never took it down or painted over it. No point in doing so since it wouldn't make the hurt go away. Instead, we just kept it as a vivid reminder, something to hold her memory and keep her here with us in a way. God, I wish that wallpaper held some answers!

"There has to be a way to repay…" I don't get to finish my sentence because he abruptly stands up and walks menacingly toward me. The man at my back releases my hair and pushes me forward so my body is almost touching Alzerro's. I stumble and fall to my knees. Alzerro holds his hand out, gesturing for me to stay below him.

"To repay me?" he says huskily, coming down on his haunches. He smells of high-end class and elegance; two things I'm not used to.

I nod my head, filtering through my thoughts for an answer to our problems. My father has borrowed money from someone who is obviously very capable of killing people, who has probably already killed many people.

"I planned on killing your father in return for my money, but since you're here, tell me what your idea is…"

The way he says idea has my skin crawling. Goosebumps erupt across my skin. I don't actually have any ideas; I just said it to try and buy us some time.

"I will get a job so we can pay you back in installments or…" I have to throw it out there. His full-on laughter cuts me off. He's an asshole, and I'm certain everyone in the room knows it. I glare at him as I watch a huge smile form on his face.

"Installments… Hmm… That's a problem, dear Bree." My name coming from his mouth causes an eruption of Goosebumps across my skin. I feel the need to ask him to keep saying it, but at the same time, the dark look he's giving me makes me want to piss and shit myself.

"Problem? I don't see what the problem is if you're being paid back. Do you?" Somehow I gain a backbone in that moment, and I stand up. I know I have every reason to be scared, but I'm not. I'm calm and cool, and I'm somehow going to find a way out of this mess. I can't lose my father, especially after just losing my mother.

I watch as Alzerro pulls a gun from his back. I'm not sure how I hadn't noticed it, and out of pure terror I fall backward, barely catching myself before I hit the floor.

"You don't make deals with the mafia, my dear. I'm the mafia king, and I don't accept installments; payments are due in full, unless they're in blood. So tell me… Who shall be paying today?" A sick smile creeps onto his face as he points the gun at my father. Alzerro's cold, dark eyes stare into mine, and there isn't an ounce of mercy there. He'll shoot my father without blinking; he'll shoot me without blinking. He isn't the type of man who gives second chances.

"No…" I beg. I'm not sure where my voice comes from. All I know is I can't face losing someone again. It will be as if I'm dead anyway.

He lowers the gun, turning his attention back on me. I can feel his hot breath on my face as he looks down at me. "What is your form of payment then?" I notice the way his eyes linger over my breasts, my body in general. He's intrigued with me. He wants me.

"Me," I whisper for his ears only. He isn't stupid; he knows what I mean. I, however, am stupid, so very fucking stupid. I know there will be no walking away from someone like him. He pushes his longish black hair from his face as he continues to hold the gun in his hand, like he's weighing his options carefully.

His eyes narrow, and for a brief second, I think he'll say no.

"Deal…" I know he isn't done, though. There's a "but" in there somewhere… "But if you run, I will kill you. Men, take care of her father." Alzerro's hand snakes out, gripping the hem of my shirt. I thought he said that we have a deal! An icy, sweaty feeling of dread sweeps through my body. This can't be happening! I only offered myself so I could save my dad! I try to push his hand away, but I'm obviously no match for him. He looks amused, yet deadly serious, as my skin feels the burn of his hand slowly roaming up to the top of my shirt. I hear the tear of fabric as he rips my shirt to gain access to my chest, but I hardly notice because I'm held captive by the fear in my father's eyes as Alzerro's men surround him.

"Stop! You said we had a deal!" I cry out. Alzerro said we have a deal, so why did he order his men to hurt my father?

I'm horrified as the thugs grip my father's head to hold him in place. The man who guided me in here looks gleeful as he takes his place next to my dad and prepares to carry out "the king's" orders. Tears stream down my dad's face as he waits for the pain to come. His eyes never leave mine, telling me how much he loves me and how sorry he is.

The brute's fist lands against my father's face with a sickening crunch. Hearing my dad's painful groans and seeing his blood gush out is just too much for me to handle, and I'm on the verge of collapsing. These thugs can't do this! They have to stop! It's wrong!

"Make them stop! Please! I will do whatever you tell me!" I'm screaming and sobbing as I plead with

Alzerro. My eyes beg for his to meet mine, but they still linger over my body. I'm close to being a hysterical, blubbering mess, but I have to keep my wits about me; I have to find strength. I have to do something. I can't lose my dad!

"Make them stop!" I implore desperately as my hands grasp his arms to get his attention and for stability before I collapse. "I already said I belong to you, that I'm my dad's payment. I'll do whatever you want. Please stop making my father suffer!"

Alzerro shrugs my hands off his arms, leaving me feeling vulnerable and unsteady. His fingers grip my chin tightly, roughly tilting my head back to force me to meet his callous stare.

"If I make them stop, you have to go with me without a problem. No fighting, no questions, and no theatrics. Do you understand?"

The second the words fall from his lips, I shake my head yes. I will do anything I can to save my father including making a deal with the devil.

"Stop," Alzerro commands. His guys immediately pull away from my father.

"Untie him and leave him be. Take her…" His eyes linger over my chest again as if he's already planning what he's going to do to me. A creepy smile spreads across his face, making my skin crawl.

"Tie her up and gag her," he orders as he runs his thumb across my bottom lip.

"I said I would go with you willingly…" My voice is weak as the men come near me. The man who retrieved me from my car roughly grabs my arm and pulls me closer to him. The other men untie and release my father. His body is so worn out, he falls off his chair and lands on the ground in a heap. Even though he has been badly beaten and is still bleeding, I know he'll be okay. It's better than being dead, after all.

"Where are you taking me?" I turn the best I can to face Alzerro. His eyes pierce mine.

"Somewhere you'll never be able to escape from." His words should scare me, and they do to some extent, but I have a feeling that I will never live more than in the moments I'm with this man.

"Are you going to kill me?" I ask foolishly. I can't help it; the question is burning a hole in my head. Another man comes up behind me to follow through with Alzerro's orders.

"Wait. Before you take me, may I please hug my dad good-bye?" I tentatively ask, hoping I can feel safe in my father's arms one last time. I'm not surprised when there's no response. Instead, my hands are tied together, causing my arms to pull together tightly. Alzerro takes a step forward while a man works rope between my legs. I don't put up any resistance. There's no point in fighting them – they are heartless, cruel assholes who won't hesitate to use their guns to kill me.

"I might be a criminal, dear Bree, but killing beautiful women isn't something I enjoy doing. If you do as you're told, I won't hurt you." His deep, silky voice invades my body and my senses. I shudder as my palms sweat, and a slick coating of fear fills my belly.

Before I'm ready, I'm being led out of my home. My heart constricts and panic seizes me as I try to look at my dad one last time. "Daddy…" I manage to gasp out before my ears fill with my dad's broken, sobbing voice. "Bree… Bree… I'm so… Bree!" My father's wails may be my final memories of him.

My throat constricts with sobs wanting to erupt, but I can't let them out. I can't break down yet, so I let anger take over my heart. When we stop at the SUVs, I turn to Alzerro with fire in my eyes and heartache in my voice. "You didn't even let me say good-bye! You didn't give me a chance to pack or take anything important to me. I have nothing, *nothing*, to remind me of my life!"

Alzerro chuckles at my outburst, and his eyes light up like he's enjoying my dismay. He fucking chuckles at me! "Oh, my darling Bree, that's kind of the point. You're mine. Your life is mine. Your memories, emotions, desires are all mine. I own you. Your life as you knew it doesn't exist anymore," he explains to me as if he's talking to a child.

It's at this moment that I realize what I've gotten myself into. As the realization quickly settles in, I make myself a promise. I will play Alzerro's game, and I will let him think he owns me. But, he'll never control my mind or my heart. He'll never know about my secret act of defiance. I will always remember who I am and where I come from. I will always be me – the Bree I want to be!

I take a deep breath, allowing my new resolve to fill me. "I know I agreed to go with you and all, but what exactly am I to do?" I hadn't even thought of that when I offered myself. I just wanted to find a way to save my father's life and get these men out of my mother's home.

"We'll start off slowly since we don't know one another. Everyday we'll work up to the best part of all…" he whispers, his breath tickling my ear.

"What's the best part?" I ask innocently.

"When you ride my dick." A smirk pulls at his lips as I gasp, and my face reddens. I'm not stupid; I know what will happen. I know someone like him doesn't just take someone like me and force her to clean his house or complete menial tasks. I just didn't expect him to be so blunt and straightforward with his words.

"Does that bother you? Riding my dick? Because you will ride it. You'll ride it long and hard. I will fill your pussy and fuck you into oblivion."

Without warning, the rope around my ankles is pulled tighter, and a scrap of fabric lands in Alzerro's hands. He leans in closer than before, and I open my mouth for him to put it in. His hands wrap the fabric around my head as he secures the gag. Then the asshole behind me tightens it even more, and my visions starts to go blurry just as my eyes land on a very pleased face. Alzerro may have gotten what he wanted, but I earned my father's freedom.

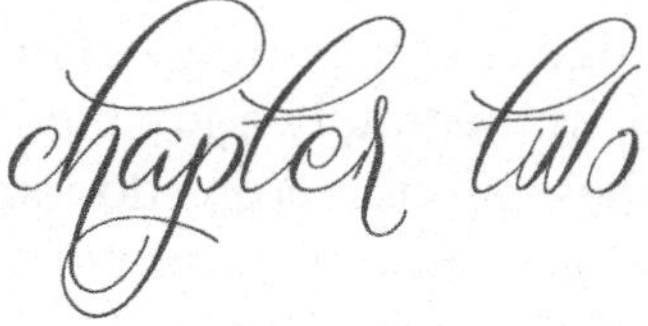

Bree

"Welcome to your new home." Alzerro's words are anything but welcoming as I enter his home…excuse me, my new fortress—it'll never be home. I massage my wrists where the rope rubbed my skin raw. My world seems fuzzy and discombobulated as I try to take everything in. I try to remember how I got here, but the last thing I remember is being gagged. Damn it, the gag must have been soaked with a sedative even though I promised I wouldn't fight him. As my wooziness dissipates, I remember my dad, the debt, me being payment...

Now I'm standing in a mafia king's home. Well, actually it's more like a mansion - the kind you see in movies that has three pools and twenty-five bedrooms, with more bathrooms than bedrooms, with live-in help... You know what I'm talking about, right?

"Thank you," I reply softly. In such a large space, my voice can hardly be heard. Just from my view in the entryway, I know this house is magnificent. The floors are marble, sleek and glistening under the lights. There's a grand, long, sweeping staircase ahead of me. I admire the high ceilings, large windows, and expensive artwork. I know seeing this house in the daylight will be amazing.

Alzerro nudges me to follow his men up the staircase. I comply immediately and quietly. We walk down a long hall, passing numerous doors. I'm not sure If I want to know what is behind them or not. We finally reach two French doors at the end of the hall.

"Leave us," Alzerro simply says. I turn around to watch his men walk away like he had ordered them to. My heart sinks into my stomach. Have I made a mistake? Did I really know what I was getting myself into?

Stop it. You didn't want them to continue hurting your father, and you know you wouldn't be able to live without him. Without your dad, you're as good as dead.

The voice in my head stops me from saying anything. I can't possibly tell this man that I'm having second thoughts, that I had no idea what I was getting myself into.

I watch as he opens the door and walks into the large room. His body relaxes as the tension within him seems to dissolve. It's like he's a completely different person in his surroundings, almost like he's really human. Almost.

"Come, *Piccolo*," he demands. *Piccolo* - is that Italian? It sounds that way, though I have no idea what it means. Without comment, I obey him and walk into his room slowly. There's a king-sized bed sitting on the far side of the room that looks like it's right out of an expensive hotel. It's large and lavish with big, fluffy pillows and beautiful, luxurious blankets.

An incredibly comfortable looking couch is centered in the middle of the room. A large television with numerous movies and games sits in front of it, and on the far wall is a desk area. However, none of these things matter nearly as much as the view that lies before me. Two French doors lead out onto a wraparound balcony.

My breath catches in my throat as I walk across the room to the open doors. The sun is setting in the distance, and the waves of the ocean break against the jagged rocks that line the shore. It's the most beautiful thing I've ever seen.

"Beautiful, isn't it?" a voice says behind me. I turn around startled, completely forgetting where I am for a moment. That is the thing about beautiful things - they can distract you for a short time, but then everything eventually turns ugly and real again.

"It's very beautiful," I reply shyly. I watch him as he heads over to his desk. He grabs a crystal bottle that is filled with a dark liquid. Two glasses clink together in his hand as I realize he's going to pour me a drink.

"No, thank you," I mutter before he can drop a splash of what I assume is bourbon. I'm not much of a drinker, not that I've had many chances to do so. I'm not even old enough to legally drink!

He turns, peering up at me. His eyes are beautiful in the setting sun. His body is lickable in so many ways, and if it's this great looking covered by his clothes, I wonder what it will look like without.

"If you insist." Alzerro pours himself a large glass and slams most of it back. A dribble escapes his mouth, landing on his full bottom lip. Right in that second I want nothing more than to lick away the sweet smelling alcohol. Except that is inappropriate, and even though he's attractive, I'm not sure I'm ready for that yet. If I make the first move, that will mean I'm ready to completely succumb to him. Then there will be nothing stopping him from taking me over and over again whenever he wants, and eventually I won't have any purpose here anymore.

Watching him more closely, I study his handsome features. His dark complexion and his dark hair and eyes tell me he's of Italian descent. His body and hands are large; his whole presence is large. I'm sure he's large in other places as well… Wait, why am I having all these inappropriate thoughts about the man who was about to kill my father over a debt but took me as payment instead? What is wrong with me? I should hate and despise this man!

"I hope you think of this place as a home, not a prison." His words are soft, and I realize he's trying to put me at ease in my new surroundings.

"I hope you treat me as a person and not a prisoner," I retort, taking a seat on the sofa and folding my hands into my lap. I don't know what else to do or where I'm supposed to go. I've been given no directions or purpose yet.

"I will treat you as you wish to be treated and no less." I gaze up into Alzerro's eyes; they are as soft as his voice. I don't know what to think or how to feel anymore. My mind is still reeling from everything that has occurred. In less than twenty-four hours, my life has changed so much.

"Thank you," I reply kindly, averting my eyes to the floor. He's intense, unlike anyone I've ever met. Looking at him causes my heart to beat abnormally fast, but not looking at him makes me feel as if I'm missing something.

"The rules are pretty simple." He purses his lips, taking the seat next to me. He waits a moment for my eyes to meet his before he continues. "You're not to run. Ever. If you do, I will kill you." My heart is beating out of my chest. Have I given up my freedom to save my father from death only to take his place?

"You cannot go outside or wander around our home; I will let you know what rooms you're allowed into. You do not speak to any of my men, but I will introduce you to the staff with whom you may converse. You'll only wear the clothes I provide and will wear what I select for special occasions. Furthermore, you're to stay in my quarters unless I say otherwise. You do NOT leave this room without my permission. You're mine to play with, to keep, and to possess." I'm breathless as he leans into my body like he's smelling me.

"And I will possess you in every single way possible," he promises, his seductive voice just above a whisper.

"What if I object?" I'm feeling very brave in that moment. I know asking this question will lead me to an answer that I don't want to hear, but I have to hear it.

"If you object, then the deal is off and is unpaid. If the debt is unpaid, then there's only one other way to pay for it, and I assure you that you don't want that to happen, *Piccolo*." His voice is dangerous, and his eyes say he isn't lying. He'll take someone's life if I do not follow his rules.

Looking down at his hands, I know he has taken many people's lives. I'm in danger of being his next victim.

"I won't object," I respond, trying my hardest to sound strong and determined. I have no other option.

"Good," he says, smiling as if he has just solved every problem in the world. The air between us is less tense now, and I find myself relaxing into the cushions more.

"Are you hungry?" Alzerro asks, swirling the bourbon in his glass. He stares into it as if all the answers to his problems lie at the bottom of the glass.

"A little," I answer shyly. I haven't eaten anything since this morning, but that's okay. I'm curvy and though that isn't a bad thing, I can lose a couple pounds.

"Anything in particular you like? I believe my cook, Silvia, made spaghetti with meatballs this evening. We could go down and get you a plate if you would like." I surprisingly find myself smiling at him. It has only been hours since I was forcefully taken from my home, the one I grew up in and lived in until the day I left for college. I viewed Alzerro as a dark, dangerous man right away, but looking at him now, I feel as if he's someone different.

"I would actually love that, please." I quickly stand at the same time he does. Our bodies brush against one another's, and an electric current flows through us. Call it fate, or whatever the hell you want, but in that zap I feel like I can read him, like he's dark and damaged for a reason. It makes me want to dig my nails into him, crawl into the dark places of his mind, and expose who he truly is.

"Let's go then." Setting his glass down, he gently grabs my hand and leads me out of the room, stopping to close and lock the door behind us. I'm not sure why he feels the need to do that being it's his house, but I'm not going to ask.

I can't help but admire Alzerro's house as we continue our journey to the kitchen. The house is large and has an elegance to it like I've never seen before. This is the type of grandeur that can't be seen anywhere - magazines can't even do it justice. It's designed and decorated to a specific standard, and I assume that standard is Alzerro King.

The kitchen is huge. Dark wood cabinets cover the walls with top of the line stainless steel appliances accompanying them. The refrigerator is the biggest I've ever seen, and the eating area is so large you could easily feed two families on Thanksgiving in it. Floor to ceiling windows take up the far wall, allowing light to come through at all angles. The floor is a white marble that probably cost more than it's worth for me to be standing on it.

I take a seat at the table, my eyes never leaving the surreal view. It's a shame someone like him has a view like this. Even if he isn't hurting me or demanding something from me now, I know it will happen sooner or later.

In a matter of minutes, a steaming hot plate sits in front of me. Red spaghetti sauce, meatballs, and noodles are the only things I can see.

"Eat it. It's amazing. This is my mother's recipe, actually." He smiles from ear to ear, but it never reaches his eyes. I can tell that there's something brewing just under his surface. He's like a hurricane, capable of taking everyone out with him once he meets the shore, so I know I need to tread carefully.

I pick up my fork, shoving a heaping bite into my mouth. I can't help but close my eyes and moan as I savor the warm deliciousness. I've never tasted anything so delectable before. When I open my eyes to take another bite, my gaze collides with Alzerro's. His eyes are dilated, and it looks as if he's about ready to jump over the table and devour me himself.

"This is really good," I compliment him. He nods at me, dismissing the look he had just given me. A coldness settles into me. I don't really want him to look at me like that, but then again, I kind of do. I feel as if I'm missing something without him, without that look.

I finish my food and stand, readying myself to wash my plate and silverware so they can be put away.

"Stop," he commands. I turn to him, my face growing red. I feel like a kid who got caught stealing cookies out of the cookie jar.

"The housekeepers take care of that." I scuff at him, not sure if I'm going to listen to him. I'm not one to allow others to clean up after me.

"I know what you're thinking. You're already thinking about disobeying me, aren't you?" It isn't really a question because I haven't done anything wrong yet, but how can cleaning up my mess be disobeying him?

"No," I lie. I refuse to tell him I'm not going to listen to him, especially over something as petty as washing my dishes after eating. My mother raised me to clean up after myself.

"Now you're lying," he remarks, taking an aggressive step in front of me. His eyes narrow as his hand snakes around my back to directly behind my neck.

His fingers dig into my skin, gripping me just above a painful level. "Never lie to me or I'll kill you." There are no emotions on his face, and his voice is cool and firm. Fear slithers up my spine and deep into my brain. It's plain to see that even the littlest things can get me killed here.

"I won't." I try my hardest to hold my chin up high. I don't want him to think that he has broken me yet. I will never be broken, though. I've lost far too much in my life to be ashamed of anything.

"Good. If you lie to me again, I will kill you. Things like that can get you killed here. Always be honest. Always." His eyes grow softer and an understanding settles over me. Honesty is huge with him. Even if it's bad honesty, he always wants to hear it.

"I will—always be honest, I mean," I stutter. I've been around him less than twenty-four hours, and I'm only here as payment for a debt, but I feel a connection to him. A pull is a better way to say it. I feel like I want to be close to him, but at the same time, I want to run away from him with all my might. It's as if he's a ticking time bomb—capable of going off at any moment.

"That's good. Honesty is always the best policy, Bree." His hand releases the back of my neck and slides down my back. With the tiniest press to the small of my back, he pushes me forward, forcing me to let the maids clean up my mess.

"In all fairness, I could really clean up my own mess, Alzerro."

"Zerro," he says.

"Pardon?" I ask in confusion, coming to a standstill.

"Zerro is what you may call me. The maids get paid to clean up after me and my guests. If you were to clean up your mess, then they would be out a job. That wouldn't be fair, would it?" That is a low blow if ever I heard one - holding one's job over someone else's head.

"That's a bit harsh, wouldn't you say?" Questioning him is a bold move for me to make. I know he doesn't owe me any answers. I'm here purely to save my father, but I can't help but ask.

"Harsh…" He laughs, but it's anything but cheery.

"I just find it harsh to hold…" My response is cut short when he gruffly grips my throat. My back lands harshly against the wooden cupboard, forcing me to stare deeply into pools of blackness. My breath expels from my chest in a rush, and I force more air in. Fear trickles in…

His hold is firm, yet I can still breathe. His other hand skims over my thigh, sending my body into overdrive. My heart beat spikes, and the fear melts into something else.

"Never question me, Bree. I could fuck and kill you faster than you could say no. I'm not a good guy; I'm not someone you should be sitting with here, talking and acting as if we're normal. We're not normal. This interaction between us isn't normal. You're merely a business transaction, a payment for a debt. That makes you about as good as the rest of the money that comes in and out of this house. Keep quiet, don't ask questions, and do as I say, and you won't be hurt." His eyes soften, and the tension rolls right off his shoulders as he releases my throat. It throbs where he held it, so I try to gently rub it.

"Come now. You must get ready for bed. I have a couple things I must take care of yet tonight." Is he really sending me to bed alone?

I follow quietly behind him, not wanting to draw more attention to myself. I wonder what it was that broke him. What it was that made him so dark and cold. But I know he isn't completely a dark soul, because every time I look in his eyes, I see a glimpse of good. Maybe that sliver of goodness will be what saves me at the end of all this.

Alzerro

"Mack, grab the gun," I brusquely order as we circle the tied up man who is now lying on my floor. Blood is dripping from his mouth, and I can see the far off look in his eyes—the one that says he knows he's going to die.

Mack hands me the gun, and I hold it firmly in my hand. A sliver of doubt pools into my mind. I've been doing this since before I was eighteen. Not once have I ever had a doubt, yet now at twenty-five, I suddenly want to feel sorry for doing this shit.

Turning my gaze to Mack again, I look at him. He's tall just like me and built like a house. Our families have been friends forever, and he's the only person I trust with my life.

He wipes the sweat from his brow as he gives me a bewildered look. I can't blame him one bit since I'm as confused as he is… Why am I still standing here with the gun in my hand? Why isn't this guy being taken away to be buried already?

"You want me to do it, Z?" Mack questions. His voice is hushed, as to not let the little snitch hear. The man who lies before me is someone who took our stash of drugs, sold them, and then took the money and ran. It wasn't the first time it has happened, and it most certainly won't be the last.

"No." I wave him off. I don't need anyone to do anything for me. I climbed my way to the top alone, and I can handle this alone too.

Squatting down, I grab the man by the chin, forcing him to look at me. "Toni, why did you have to go and pull a stupid stunt like this?" There's nothing sincere about my questioning. It's mocking, taunting even. See, I like it when these people try to fight back because it makes me feel that much more powerful.

He doesn't say anything to me; in fact, it seems as if he's looking straight through me rather than at me. This just pisses me off even more.

"Any last wishes?" I ask smirking, the gun cocked and ready. I generally never take this long to put a bullet in someone's head, but something is off about me tonight. I can feel it.

Bree.

My mind whispers her name faintly. I grip the gun more firmly in my hand. The man says nothing to me, so I take that as his answer. Putting the gun to his head, I kiss his forehead and pull the trigger. The ringing that is generally associated with shooting a gun no longer affects me. I can't tell you how many people I've killed with this gun alone. After a while, your body just gets used to it.

I stand up, wiping the splattered blood from my dress shirt. I turn around, taking notice of Mack's eyes on me.

"What?" I question. This isn't something he hasn't seen before. He should've been pulling the body out of the house by now, not standing here looking at me like a baffled fucker.

He points up to the balcony where Bree is standing. Even from this distance, I can see the shock and disbelief in her eyes. Did she honestly not take my warnings seriously? Is she dumb enough to think that I won't kill her?

Handing Mack my gun, I dart up the stairs to my room. Anger is obvious in every step I take. Obviously I need to teach her a lesson. She needs to learn that my word always matters and must always be obeyed.

The second my foot touches the top step, I hear the door to my room click closed. Did she think that I wouldn't know? I forcefully push through the door. It slams against the wall, but I don't even care. I don't care about scaring her or breaking shit. All I care about is her learning to listen and obey what I say.

"Didn't I tell you to stay in here?" I angrily ask her, already knowing the answer. She's sitting on the far side of the bed, her face hidden behind a mess of brown hair.

My voice is heard only by myself, though, because she doesn't look up. This only throws more gasoline onto the fire. Maybe I need to remind her who is in charge…

I walk over to my desk to grab my favorite gun before I cross the room and grip her arm, pushing her down onto the bed. Her eyes grow even wider with fear as she takes notice of the gun.

"I didn't…" she stutters. It doesn't matter what she did - I don't want to hear it. I place the barrel of the gun against her lips, making her fully aware of what I can do, *will do*, to her.

"I don't care about your excuses. When I tell you to stay put, I mean it. It's not for shits and giggles, Bree. This world isn't the world you're used to." Every word that slips from my mouth is laced with some sort of self-induced anger. Rationally, I know I have no real reason to be mad at her, but it pisses me off that she didn't listen.

Tears prick at the corners of her eyelids and slide down her cheeks. I feel my heart beat. Once. It beats once in that second as I watch more tears slip from her eyes.

Pulling the gun from her lips and setting it on the night stand, I stand to my full stature. She's still looking at me like I just killed a bucket full of kittens.

"Why did you kill him?" she asks quietly, as if she really doesn't mean to ask it at all. She looks down at the floor, her brown hair flowing around her head like she just brushed it. She's wearing a pair of plaid pajama bottoms and a white spaghetti strap tank top. She looks so young and naïve. I almost want to wrap her up and send her away, as far away from me as I can get her. But I won't, simply because I'm too selfish to.

"He deserved to die." It's that simple. I untuck my dress shirt from my slacks, pulling at the buttons to take it off.

"People don't just deserve to die." Her voice is no longer that of the meek girl I had just seen. I smile to myself for the strength that she's showing. It will be a pleasure to break her.

"They do when they owe me money, even more so when they steal from me. He stole from me and took my money. Not that any of this concerns you." I sound like an asshole. Even though I have no reason to justify my actions, I feel like I have to. I feel like I need her to understand why I did what I did.

"Did you ever think he needed the money? Maybe he was poor and had a family he just wanted to feed and clothe?" Her voice is pitched, and her face is etched in anger. I want to be proud that she has a backbone, but I also want to break it, snapping it into itty-bitty pieces. People with her attitude don't make it very long where I come from.

"Generally, anyone who comes to me needs the money. It doesn't matter what it's for, Bree. If you make a deal with the devil for your soul and lose, he'll take it. Well, in this case I'm the devil. They made the deal; I was just following through with the soul taking part."

Her nose tips up, and her eyes grow with a fire that makes my dick ache. Maybe taking her wasn't the best idea…

"You're a monster. A sick, horrific monster who gets off on using and abusing people." The distaste in her voice only makes me want her more. A smile pulls at my lips as I pull my shirt off completely. Her eyes go straight to my bare chest and stay there for a moment. Even if she thinks I'm a monster, she's still attracted to me.

"Ahhh, continue telling me how much of a monster I am. Please," I mockingly plead, tilting my head at her. She narrows her eyes, and her tongue dips out of her mouth and onto her bottom lip to moisten it. She looks like a snake ready to strike.

Her eyes leave mine as she adjusts herself in the bed, her body rolling over as she pulls the covers up and over her head. I must have misread her. I thought for sure she was going to strike back with something.

"Are we done playing games already?" I taunt her, walking over to the bed and sliding into my spot. She scoots closer to her side, as if getting away from me is her number one priority. That's too bad because getting closer to her is *my* number one priority.

Reaching out, I put my hand under the blanket and latch onto her arm. A squeal escapes her mouth as I pull her toward me. Of course she has to fight me. Of course it makes me want her more.

"Let. Go. Of. Me," she grits out every word as she tries to shake me off. Does she think she can win? Does she think I won't hurt her? I will…

I won't...

"Nope." I pull harder until she's on my side of the bed, and I'm leaning over her. Our chests are pushed against one another's, and her breaths are coming in at a rate that is way higher than normal…

"Stop," she breathes out. It suddenly dawns on me that I know nothing about her, nothing other than her father owes me quite a bit of money. However, I'm enjoying our current interaction way too much to think much of it.

"Why?" I ask, cocking my head. I'm not touching her, at least not like I want to be touching her.

"I don't even know you. We don't know each other."

I laugh a full-on belly-shaking laugh. "Then why the fuck would you even volunteer to come with me? You do realize that you, well, mostly your body, will be paying your father's debt, don't you? Every moan, groan, orgasm, and every spread of those legs will be payment." Her eyes dilate as her breaths become pants. She couldn't have been that far gone; she had to have known that she would be coming here for so much more than just helping me.

Suddenly, she finds her voice. "I didn't have any other option. I would rather be taken than lose my only other parent." Something about what she says tugs at my heart and pulls me out of the haze that is consuming me. I can tell myself over and over again that I don't have a heart, but every word that comes from her mouth reminds me that I do.

"Roll over and go to sleep," I grudgingly command, standing from the bed. She looks at me in confusion, wrinkles marring her beautiful face. I will admit that she's beautiful, unlike anything I'm used to. Her face is soft, her cheeks full, and she radiates youthfulness. Her nose is small, and her teeth are straight and white. She's simple, but at the same time not so simple you wouldn't notice her.

"Did I finally hit a sore spot?" she taunts, sitting up from her lying position. It's strange seeing a woman in my bed.

"No. You merely reminded me that I can't care for wounded, sick, little puppies like yourself." It's a knee jerking reaction to fire back a shitty remark.

"I'm not a wounded, sick puppy. I'm a girl who lost her mom to cancer and is doing her father a favor because she doesn't want him to die." Her indignant voice echoes off the ceiling and rings in my ears. My veins fill with acid as I stalk over to her. She's small and innocent, but she's prey and is lying in my bed.

"Did you just yell at me?" I ask coolly.

"I didn't just yell at you. I told you exactly what I had wanted to since you tied me up in my home." This time she's the one radiating coldness.

"Shut up," I grit out. She's getting on my last nerve, and the only way I know how to deal with things that get on my nerves is to kill them. Except I can't kill her. I made a deal, and I'm a man of my word.

"No. You shut up. You bring me to this house, and I have no idea what's going on or who you are. You take my entire world away from me, leaving me at your mercy. I'm confused, scared, and trying to figure out how I should approach all of this and you…" I cut her off, my lips sending whatever words that were going to escape back into her.

A groan escapes her lips, and I smile against her mouth knowing full well she enjoys my lips on hers. I coax her lips open, slowly invading her mouth with my tongue. She tastes delectable, and I feel as if I won't ever be able to get enough of her.

Her small hands skim across my chest and onto my back. Her nails rake my skin, and I'm on verge of losing the last shred that is holding me back from taking her on the very first night she's here.

Pulling back, I take in the red splotches spreading across her cheeks as her big, brown, doe eyes look back at me. She looks thoroughly satisfied.

"Not so much of a monster now, am I?" I joke, my finger swiping across her plump bottom lip.

"You're still a monster…" she retorts, pulling away from me as if she's embarrassed to have kissed me and enjoyed it.

"Remember that, sweetheart, when I bury my face between those creamy thighs of yours," I smirk. I think I hear her gasp as I walk away, but it could've been my imagination. Now I have to take a shower, so I can beat myself off. There's no way I'm taking her on her first night here. I might be heartless, but I still care... At least a little bit.

When I awake the next morning, my body is overly warm. I feel a small hand against my chest and a leg curved into my thigh. Even if she says she hates me, this alone tells me that she craves something—comfort.

I turn to glare at the clock that sits on the nightstand. It's nearly six a.m., and though I don't normally get up this early, I feel like I need to. I have some built up aggression, and I can't get through the day if I don't go work out.

I slip quietly and slowly from the bed, so I don't wake Bree. She's a spitfire. I haven't given her enough credit. She isn't okay with anything that I do; in fact, I'm sure she's afraid of it—she should be. The mafia is no place for a woman. My mother hadn't…

The thought enters my mind, but I force it away. I refuse to think about my mother. Refuse. It's a shame because I loved her, but thinking about her opens up a gaping hole in my chest.

"Sir, there's someone here to see you," Mack announces over the intercom that is located in my bathroom. I slip into the closet and pick out a pair of low-rise blue jeans and a T-shirt. I plan on staying home today, so I pick something that is laid back.

"I'll be down in five," I reply. I wipe on some deodorant and brush my teeth.

Then I slip out of the bedroom, but not before I allow myself a second to look at Bree lying in my bed. I feel nothing for her, but at the same time I do. We both lost our mothers, so I know what she's going through on that front, but everything else is foreign to me.

"Who the fuck is here this early?" I yell to Mack, descending the stairs two at a time. My foot hits the bottom step when I turn to the front door to see Luccio. He's the mafia leader a city over. We have no bad blood between us, but that doesn't make it okay for him to come into my house without being invited.

"Luccio," I greet him calmly. He's wearing a buttoned down shirt and dress slacks. He doesn't look as if he's ready to spill blood, but most criminals don't fit the profile of one.

"Alzerro," he responds. His words are heavily laced with an Italian accent that reminds me of home.

"Mack tells me you're here for something. What can I help you with?" I question, raising an eyebrow at him.

He looks between Mack and me before dismissing his men. I'm not sure what is meant by that, but I don't ask questions. A bat of my eyelash sends Mack away to tend to other needs in the house.

"I believe we have gotten onto a case that you may want to know about." What could Luccio possibly be talking about? We walk the short distance to the sitting room, taking seats across from one another.

"Continue… I'm listening." And I am. Intently.

"We believe one of your men and one of my men have been working together for some time, without it being known by either side. We also believe that they have information in regards to your mother's death."

The way he says my mother's death makes it seem real, and I hate seeing it like that. I clench my fists tightly together to stop myself from lashing out at him.

"What do you mean? You either have the proof that such things are taking place or you don't."

He runs a hand through his greying hair. He reminds me so much of my father in the way he talks and stands and in his gestures and mannerisms… If he wasn't from another mafia family, I would consider him to be my own blood.

"See, that's the problem, Alzerro. We have nothing other than a tip that led us to a dead body. This is the mafia, and you know about us much as we do. Our people know how to kill - we train them, teach them to do so. They will kill every lead we get, and they'll disappear right from under our noses."

He's right. Fuck it. He's right. I run a hand through my hair, hoping it will ease some of the tension out of me. There's too much going on right now between the girl upstairs, this, and the many debts that need to be settled…

"Luccio," I sigh.

"Alzerro, I know you're a busy man. I wouldn't have come to you if I didn't believe this information. I'm trying to look out for the best of both of our kingdoms, *Fratello*." I know he means it out of the kindness of his heart. No one else has ever called me his brother.

"I understand that. I truly do. But you do understand what accusing our own kind does, don't you?" I had to ask him. It will cause an uprising if anyone discovers what we're planning to do. If it's discovered that we're wrong, we would be seen as weak, and weak in the mafia just gives people another reason to take you out.

A smile tips at his lips. "Yes, young Alzerro, I do. Have you forgotten your father and I worked together?"

"No, I haven't," I say, returning his smile. The mafia is my family. My men are my family. That's just how it works.

"Good. I will keep you updated. I just want you to watch your men and do so diligently. We will smell 'em out, and when we do, I have a bullet with their names on it." I can see the determination in his eyes.

I nod my head. "Yes. If I find anything out, I will give you a call." He stands suddenly, bending down to place a kiss upon my forehead. It's meant out of respect.

"Thank you for seeing me," Luccio says before he leaves with his men following behind him like bloodhounds.

"What was that about?" Mack comes into the sitting room after closing the door behind them. He looks a bit leery of me, and it then occurs to me: Should I tell him? Should I let him in on the secret that Luccio is on the case of finding my mother's killer? That it might be one of our own men?

"Luccio thinks there may be a pig among us. Came by to let me know," I lie. Well, half lie. I can't possibly tell him everything, even if I trust him. In this line of business, no one can ever be fully trusted. Lines can never be drawn, or they will be crossed daily. It's best to keep things to yourself.

"Well, if I hear anything among the men, I will let you know," Mack assures me.

"Thank you," I reply, dismissing him. The fact that my mother's killer is out there, possibly beneath one of two families is far too much for me to stomach. I find myself crawling back upstairs to my bathroom to take another shower.

It's funny how I can kill left and right and pull people from their families like nothing, yet something so simple can bring me to my knees. It doesn't matter how much I say I don't care, or how much I try to bathe in the blood of those I kill; it never takes the pain away, never makes me forget.

Bree

When I awake, I'm alone. The spot next to mine in the bed is cold, and I sigh in relief. There's no way I can handle waking up next to him. My heart is beating out of my chest as it is. I want to see him, but at the same time I don't. I hate him, but I kind of find him endearing at the same time.

His smirk makes my insides melt, but his cockiness and the way he handles things make me want to turn his gun on him. I can hear the shower running in the bathroom. I need to pee but feel it's safer to hold it. I take the small amount of time I have alone to think things over.

Alzerro, or Zerro, or whatever the hell he calls himself, told me he would kill me over and over again yesterday. I don't think he'll ever kill me, though, not even after I watched him kill that man on the floor downstairs yesterday. I can't stop feeling like I need to help Zerro in some way, despite the fact I hardly know him.

Then there's the fact that I'm not sure why I'm really here. He didn't take me last night; in fact, he stayed on his side of the bed while I stayed on mine. I know it won't last long, though. One way or another, I will have to spread my legs for him. I will have to give him access to who I am.

The water turns off and the door opens, pulling me from my thoughts. I watch him as he walks out of the bathroom with a scrap of a towel covering his lower half. It looks more like a washcloth covering the area, but who am I kidding? All I can think about is the way his mouth felt against mine last night and how his abs… God, his abs are beautiful…each chiseled, little marking on his stomach…the dips and planes and that V… That fucking V is something women would kill over.

"Let me give you something more to stare at…" His sultry voice pulls me out of my trance only to throw me back into it as he drops the towel from his waist.

I can't help my expression. My eyes widen, and my mouth gapes open. A family of flies could have made my mouth their home, it's open so long. I snap it closed, hoping he doesn't see my awe and desire. He's very well hung. His head has beads of water on it yet, and he's cleanly shaven.

"Do you like?" he asks, smirking. His hand strokes the base, and I swear to God one of my ovaries explodes. Pulling my eyes from his…cock to his eyes turns me into a puddle of mush. I know he just killed a guy yesterday, and he's all kinds of fucked up, and I'm supposed to be paying a debt for my father, but I'm attracted to him. I can't help it, and I'm not sure if I want to.

I don't respond to his question, afraid that it will come out as a moan. Instead, I get out of bed and head straight to the bathroom as I listen to his laughter.

"You can't hide from it, *Piccolo*." His voice has an amusement to it that hadn't been there yesterday. I sit on the toilet to take care of my business. I'm afraid he'll come barging in, but believe he'll actually respect my privacy. One can't tell with him.

"My dick calls to you…" Now he's just being an ass. A smile pulls at my lips, though. As fucked up as all this is, and it's all kinds of fucked up, it's nice to smile just a little bit even if I have no clue what will happen to me today since I'm staying with someone who points a gun at people more often than he talks.

I wipe, flush, and wash my hands before actually taking a look at myself in the mirror. I feel fine, though my cheeks are lightly flushed. My eyes are a warm brown, shining back at me. My hair needs some serious taming, but other than that, I don't look as if I've been taken by a mafia king into an unknown, evil land. The fact that he's still out there, probably naked, reminds me that I need to take my birth control. The man can get me pregnant with one look.

I come out of the bathroom and peek around the corner, waiting for him to jump out at me. When I spot him sitting at his desk with at least a pair of jeans on, I sigh in relief.

I pad across the floor, hoping that he's too engrossed in his mafia shit to care what I'm doing.

"Come here, *Piccolo*," he says sternly. I stop dead in my tracks before turning around to face him. His hair is a mess with water droplets still clinging to it, and his face looks less dark, though he still seems to have an edge to him. His demeanor seems to warn if you get too close, he'll cut you straight down the middle without a moment's hesitation.

"What does that even mean?" I ask, proceeding toward him with caution. He watches every step I take, his eyes going from my feet to the top of my head.

"It doesn't matter what it means." I can tell he isn't going to answer me, so I let it go.

"Then don't call me it. My name is Bree," I retort. For some unknown reason, I find my voice. I don't want to be that weak girl who cowers in the corner because she's scared. I need to deal with the situation. That's what my momma would have told me to do: Grab the bull by its horns.

"I will call you whatever the fuck I want. Now drop your pants and panties and sit on the edge of the desk." His finger points at the exact location my butt cheeks need to be. Instead of doing as he wants me to do, though, I glare at him, willing ice daggers to come out of my eyes and stab him.

"No," I say in the same cold tone he had given me. A fire ignites in his eyes, and I wonder if that's what gets him off: killing people and sex.

"No?" he questions, raising his eyebrow.

"No. As in N.O." I spell it out for him in case he doesn't understand I don't want to have sex with him yet. Not that there's shit I can do about it, but I still try.

"Okay…" he says smiling. It's a dazzling one; you know the kind that makes you go all weak in the knees? Yeah, that one. I'm so caught up in it that I don't notice his body moving, or that he's within a breath's distance from grabbing me. Picking me up, he pulls my pants and panties down to my ankles and places my ass on the cold wood of his desk.

"No!" I shriek, holding my legs together. If he wants something from me, he'll have to take it because I'm not giving him anything.

He smiles again, pulling my pants and panties from my ankles so my legs can move freely.

"Yes," he growls, his hands gripping my upper thighs.

"No," I counter back with the same amount of intensity. "I refuse to have sex with you."

His hands skim up my thighs and up my stomach until one is tilting my chin up to him, and the other is playing with a lock of my hair.

"I won't fuck you yet," he says softly, his breath tickling my face, and it's then, when we're nose to nose, that I can see gold flakes in his eyes. They almost make him look like a lion.

"What will you do then?" I'm not naïve. Sure, I'm young and still very much a virgin, but I'm not stupid. I've made out with boys and let them feel me up, but it never went as far as I am now: naked from the waist down.

"I need to release some tension and instead of calling a high class whore, I figured I have you here, so why not use you…" *Use me*. The words make acid build up in my stomach. He leans forward, his teeth nipping at my bottom lip.

A spark of pain and pleasure shoots straight to my core. He's fire to my insides, igniting something inside of me that I've never felt before, even though it feels wrong, and being used is something I don't want. His lips feel right. His hands on me feel right. Our hearts beating as one feels even more right.

"Let me..." he begs, his kisses on my neck causing my chest to feel feverish. I can't tell which way is up or down, and a burning feeling is settling into my core. All I can do is nod my head in response. He lays me down, kissing a small path over my neck before lifting my shirt and blazing a fire of kisses across my stomach.

Once I realize he's going further south, all the fuzzy feelings leave me. I've never had that done before, and I'm not sure I want to try it now. I clam up, but my insides are still burning with need. I don't know what to do because there's no way my legs are spreading. At this moment, I hate being so inexperienced.

Zerro obviously notices my hesitation as he pulls away, his eyes seeking mine.

"I haven't ever…" I trail off, completely embarrassed with myself and lack of sexual conquests.

He smiles, and I'll be damned if my insides don't jump up and down. "It's okay. I will be careful; I promise I won't hurt you. Just let me in…" His breath is deliciously hot against my skin. I know, even if he doesn't say it, that this is part of the agreement, that I came with him for this.

Spreading my legs, just the slightest bit, I bite my lip hard to stop myself from crying out. The simplest movements have me on edge.

He looks down at me, a hunger so deep and primal within him that I wonder if he has changed into an animal.

His eyes linger over my pussy before coming back up to mine.

"You're beautiful and untainted… You really are mine in every…single…way." His fingers separate my folds before I hear him drop to his knees. All I can feel is his hot breath on my entrance. I close my eyes as confusion and lust fill every pore of my body. I can't help but feel like I'm betraying myself. I admit that I want him, but to want him this badly after all that he has done, after only knowing him a short time… Is it wrong?

I'm not given the chance to answer my own question. His tongue slips between my folds as he gives me a full lick from bottom to top. Biting my lip hard, I try my hardest to not let my pleasurable moan escape, but some of it does.

"Tell me, does this feel good?" he enquires, his thick finger entering me slowly, so slowly that it almost hurts.

"Ahhh…" This is all I can verbalize as he slides in and out of me so slowly I would much rather have him put that gun to my head again.

"Or this?" His tongue dives in as he pumps in and out of me. He sucks my clit into his mouth while nipping on it tenderly. I'm on the very edge, but he somehow stops me from coming.

"Please…" I pant out. My hands go straight to his hair. It's soft and makes me want to do so many more things than what we're currently doing.

"Am I a monster, *Piccolo*?" His voice is just above a whisper. When I don't answer him, I hear him growl and feel his assault on my clit.

"Yes… Yes… Yes!" I scream. I'm so close to getting my release. I feel myself growing wetter with every slip of his finger inside me.

"I am?" he questions with amusement in his voice. He's having fun torturing me, and that alone makes him a monster. His finger withdraws from me only to be replaced by his tongue. He swirls it around, dipping it in and out, never giving me enough…

"I'm dying…" I groan. I feel as if I'm dying since my body is on the verge of climaxing, but he won't let me get there.

"Death, *Piccolo*, wouldn't be nearly as peaceful or pleasurable," he purrs against my clit, giving it one last tug before he inserts two fingers inside me. He pulls his face away as he places one hand on my lower abdomen and uses his other to plow his fingers in and out of me.

"Fuuuuuck…"

"Yes?"

"Yes… Yes… Yes…" I feel my ass cheeks sliding across his desk. The intensity of his thrusting with me pushing against him pushes me over the edge. My insides clench, and the burning consumes me as a deep warmth radiates gloriously throughout my body.

I feel myself falling back down to earth. My eyes are heavy, and every part of my body feels as if I've been through the wringer. I smile blissfully. He may be an evil man, someone who kills people with his hands and guns, but he definitely knows how to pleasure a woman. He can cause you extreme pain or bring you to great lengths of pleasure.

"Coming back down to earth, *Piccolo*?" he teases, his tongue running across my stomach, dipping into my belly button. I tense as my body continues to reel with aftershocks. I can't handle anymore, and I whimper as I pull my legs together.

"You're a monster…" I snarl, sitting up. I take in his messy hair and the dashing smile on his face. His eyes twinkle with darkness, need, and even a want deep within. I smile smugly to myself when I realize I affect him this way.

"I am. This I already know. I possess the tools to kill someone with pain or pleasure." His words are like silk to my insides, melting me over and over again. He doesn't even have to touch me. This is dangerous; he's dangerous.

The papers that were on his desk have fallen to the floor. I gaze down at his jeans. They are undone, but his cock is still tucked inside. I can see the outline of it bulging, begging to be released. I've given a blow job a time or two in my day, nothing compared to what he has probably already received, but it feels wrong to receive and not give.

Slipping from the desk, I drop to my knees. The plush carpet against my legs makes me shiver. His smile slips as I tug his jeans down and release him. His cock springs free like a caged animal.

I bite my lip and then lick him from base to tip. He smells of soap and all man. It's enticing and makes my blood sing. I've never been bad, never done anything wrong in my life, but this man has me wanting to cross off a whole list of bad things.

"Take me…" he rumbles, his hand wringing into my hair as he pulls it tightly. It stings, almost painfully, but at the same time it shakes me to the core. I watch him carefully as my lips slip over his cock, taking almost all of him into my mouth. My tongue swirls around the head. His teeth grit, his jaw clenching under pressure.

I can't help but reach up and trace the planes of his stomach. His muscles constrict with every lick and suck from my mouth.

"Sei e' angelo." His words are a whisper, and though I'm not sure what he says, it sounds beautiful. I take him deeper into my mouth until he's hitting the back of my throat with precision. His hands clutch my hair tightly, keeping my face up to his. We stare into one another's eyes until I feel his balls tightening and his movements become jerky.

His eyes close, and for one tiny minute in time, I get to see a part of him that is peaceful, that shows insecurity. For a moment, he's stripped of all the other things that he'll be for the day. Right now he's mine, and I'm okay with that.

Hot semen hits the back of my throat, and though it tastes absolutely disgusting, I swallow every last drop.

He smiles at me like a devil who has stolen my soul. "I underestimated the hold you have on people. On me." He says the words out loud, but it seems as if he's talking to himself.

"You're very welcome, Alzerro," I mock him, coming to stand next to him. His eyes flare with anger and something else, something deep within. I just can't place the look.

"You should be thanking me." I cock an eyebrow. Is this man ever not so full of himself?

"I shouldn't be thanking you. We should be thanking each other," I respond haughtily. Turning on my heels, I go over to my new closet to find something to wear. Generally, I'm modest and shy about my body, but he has already seen my goodies, and his tongue has tasted them…

When I come out with my clothes in hand, he's still standing there staring at me. His finger, the one he dipped inside me over and over again, is in his mouth. He's sucking on it.

"You taste better than some of the finest wines I've had." His voice is low, and the room smells of sex. I'll be damned if every thought about not letting him fuck me flies out the window.

"Do I?" I question.

"Yes… And I'm sure you'll only taste better as time goes on." Time stands still between us. His words only cause the ache inside of me to grow. My body begs for him, but my mind—my mind knows how fucked up all this is.

"Guess you'll never know, will you?" I'm baiting him. This game is fire. He's dangerous, and I know he can go off at any time.

"Don't play games with me. Get dressed. I have somewhere I need to take you." His words are a command. I reach for my clothes to get dressed without thinking. He has that much power...

My body hums with anticipation. It has been hours since I've last seen Zerro. He left me breathless and hot and bothered standing in his room. My hands drift over the tight satin fabric that clings to my body. When he told me to get ready, that we had to go somewhere, I didn't expect to be dressed up.

I've never looked this sexy in my entire life. My hair is in loose curls that fall softly down my back. The dress is black satin and sparkles in the light. A sweetheart neck line and tight bodice show off every curve.

My makeup is done to perfection; a smoky eye gives way to accenting my eyes. Looking in the full length mirror, I hardly recognize myself.

"Don't fret, you look beautiful." His voice is commanding as it always is, pulling everything in the room to his attention.

Still looking in the mirror, I skim a finger across my chest. It's creamy white, and I worry I will stick out like a sore thumb in this black dress.

I turn around, becoming very aware of his presence. He's standing before me in a charcoal grey suit with a white dress shirt underneath. The first couple buttons are undone, and I can't pull my eyes from his exposed piece of flesh.

"You're to be on your best behavior tonight. Understand?' He pulls the side of his suit jacket over to show me his gun. It's a warning: if I act out, he isn't afraid to use it. The look in his eyes tells me he will.

"I will be…" I murmur.

"Good," he replies, smiling as he leads me out the door and down the stairs. His men are dressed similarly to him, but they are wearing ties, blood red ties. I don't find that as a mere coincidence as I'm sure blood will be spilled this evening.

We all assemble to the black SUVs. Zerro and I are ushered into the middle one while his men get in the other ones. Mack joins us, his eyes clinging to me, making me feel beyond uncomfortable.

Zerro seems cool and collected as he stretches his limbs and slides into the seat next to me. It's as if a mask slips onto his face. I'm starting to understand there's a difference between business Zerro and pleasure Zerro.

"Mack, let the men know we're on our way." His voice is firm and assertive.

"Yes, sir," Mack simply responds, never questioning him. I sit in my seat fidgeting with my hands, unsure why I'm going with them. Is there a reason? Is he going to whore me out to his friends? Kill me? Fear trickles into my stomach, eating away at all the warm, fuzzy feelings he inspired this morning.

His phone rings in his pocket, and I look at him as he reaches into his pocket to pull it out. He swears under his breath before pushing a button on the screen.

"Why are you calling me, Luke?" Zerro's voice is venomous, causing my heart to shake in my chest. I avert my eyes to stare out the window, not wanting to see the man I met this morning disappear.

"I don't fucking care! You bring all of them with you. Every single last one. If they don't have the money, I will put a bullet in their heads. Got it?"

Whatever Luke says calms him slightly, but when I look back over at him, one of his hands is sunk deeply into his dark locks. He's frustrated.

"No. If you don't do as I say, I'll have a bullet with your name on it too." Luke isn't given a chance to respond because the phone is thrown across the seat.

"Sir… I can try to figure out what's wrong." Mack is trying to be helpful, or so it seems. Concern is etched into his features, but it appears fake to me in a way. He's tall, dark, and incredibly handsome. His features are very similar to Zerro's, and for a second I wonder if they are related.

"No," Zerro says firmly. Mack turns in his seat, his eyes catching mine in the rearview mirror. There's a warning, not the kind that says if you do something, I'll hurt you, but one that says be careful, tread lightly.

No fucking way will I be shining a spotlight on myself. I want to get out of this alive. The ride couldn't have been more than twenty minutes, but it seems like an eternity while I'm in the car with Zerro. The tension comes off of him in waves, and I can tell he's fuming angry. I'm terrified by this man.

Everyone pours from the vehicles, and when I get out, I look around. I think we're at some kind of night club. A long line of partiers stands before us - women and men of all shapes and sizes. I'm wobbly on my feet as Zerro presses his hand firmly on the small of my back.

"You don't have to be an asshole to me just because you're mad at someone else…" I whisper for his ears only, feeling as if I'm running to keep up with his pace.

He smiles, a tiny one. "I have to be an asshole at all times. Weakness is showing mercy to others. I can't let these people see that."

We pass the line of people, and we're let through by a big, muscular guard dressed in all black. He looks like he fights for a living. He stamps something on my hand, and we're on our way.

Through the doors, I hear the music pounding and see lights swirling in different directions in various colors. Anticipation and excitement builds in me to be in there dancing and singing, but I'm pulled away instead. Zerro ushers me to the right and down a long hall until we come to a door.

"We aren't going dancing?" I ask bashfully. I'm confused, to say the least.

"Business first." His voice is emotionless, and because the hall is so dark, I can't see his face. He presses firmly against my back, leading me down the stairs.

"Everyone against the wall!" I hear someone below us shout. My body locks up when my heels hit the bottom step, and I take in the scene before me.

People of all ages, colors, and ethnicities stand against the wall of a cold, dank, dark room.

Giving me a soft push, Zerro leads us out onto the cement floor. All eyes are on us, and all I want to do is run to the nearest exit.

"Welcome. I hear many of you have failed to come up with the money that you owe to my family." The devil has come out to play. I know it and so do all the other people in the room. Their faces morph into undeniable fear in front of me.

"You see Toni, a beloved salesman of mine, was found stealing from me. STEALING!" he yells, his words echoing off the walls. I find myself backing up with every word that falls from his lips. Instead of hitting the wall, I fall against a warm chest.

Mack. His hands clamp onto my shoulders, holding me firmly in place.

"Do you know what I did to him?" The dim lighting makes it hard to see his face, but as he reaches for his gun, I catch a glimpse of it in the light. His face is hard, dark, and cold. Evil, pure evil.

No one says a word. It's pin-drop quiet. I know this is just the wake before the storm. He'll end all their lives, and for that, he has no soul.

"I killed him. You know why?" His gun is being swung in every direction, and had Mack not clamped onto me, I would have been running up the stairs by now.

"Because the money was mine. MINE! He was supposed to deal for me and give me the money he made. It seems as if some of you've decided to follow in his footsteps."

Zerro's footsteps can be heard crossing the concrete floor until he stops in front of a middle aged man. His hair is slick with grease like it hasn't been washed in several weeks, and his eyes are red and jittery. He looks as if he's waiting for his next hit.

"Is that what you do, Zach?" Zerro questions, his words coming out like a verbal slap.

Zach doesn't answer, though. He simply stares ahead, waiting for his time to come, probably already knowing that he has no chance of surviving Zerro's wrath.

"No answer?" Zerro cocks his head to the side, mocking him. It's sick and twisted, and I worry that if I have to watch even one more second of this degrading shit, I will puke all over the floor.

Silence falls before the booming sound of a gun being fired fills the air. My ears ring fiercely as I become slightly disoriented. I watch between blurred eyes as he walks to another person, his gun pointed at point blank range.

A woman in the corner begins crying. Her body is shaking while she says a prayer in a language I don't understand. I watch Zerro cross the floor and come to a stop directly in front of her. She draws back from him as much as she can since the wall is directly behind her. He's truly the devil in human form.

"You cower in fear, yet days ago you came begging to me, pleading that you needed help." His voice is raising with every word that leaves his mouth. "Yet, here you are now, pleading and begging not to die. People like you will beg and plead for everything their whole lives."

I'm not sure how much more I can take. If I can stand idly by while watching him tear these people to shreds, what type of person does that make me?

"We have children…families," the woman sobs. She could be a single mother or a college student. Her mother could be dying, and she could be doing everything in her power to stay afloat. That single thought forces so much anger into me that I'm seeing red.

"Stop this insanity right now!" I scream at Zerro. My voice doesn't shake, and I'm not afraid to stand up to him. I don't know how, but I'm filled with an inner strength that spurs me to try and help these people.

He spins around so quickly, my head is reeling. Mack gives me a harsh shake, as if to say shut your mouth, you crazy bitch. But it isn't me who is crazy. Zerro's eyes zero in on me like I'm prey. With precision, he crosses the room, his body gliding across the ground. I should be scared, I should be begging, pleading, crying, wanting nothing but mercy from him. I'm not, though. I'm standing tall, and I will look him straight in the eyes and tell him what a crazy fuck he is.

His fingers dig into my arm painfully as he drags me out into the center of the basement so all eyes are on us. I don't even try to stop him since I know it will be useless.

His scent surrounds me, making me forget where we are for a second.

All those things disappear the moment I feel the warmth against my skin. The barrel of his gun is pointed at the side of my head, and for one tiny second, I wonder if he'll actually pull the trigger this time.

Pain registers in my mind as he grips me harder, twisting me around to face him. His eyes are black, and there's a bleak chance that I will not walk away from this.

"Does anyone want to explain to this girl what happens when someone defies me?" My heartbeat skyrockets and is the only thing I can hear in my ears. Everything else seems far away as I stare into a pair of eyes that see nothing but death.

The room remains silent, and I don't dare look away from him. It's as if it's a contest to see who will give mercy first. I feel the determination and compassion my mother instilled in me strengthening me.

"You cannot kill all these people simply because they owe you money," I grind out. It's a whisper, but I know he hears me. I know he understands what I'm saying.

My words mean nothing to him, though. I know it the moment he throws me to the ground. My body falls hard as my head smacks off the concrete. My vision blurs when the popping noises begin like a machine gun going off. I hear their screams but am in too much pain to get up. Instead, I roll over to look up. What I see causes my heart to break. My stomach coils in pain as I hold back the vomit that wants to escape.

Blood splatters across the walls as bodies sag to the ground. He shoots every single person. My body goes limp as tears spill from my eyes. How can someone be so fucked up? So uncaring? They were human too.

A hand reaches out, gripping my arm and pulling me to a standing position. I can't respond to anything, can't process the cruelty surrounding me. My mind is off in la-la-

land, and my body isn't responding. I feel as if I'm outside of my body watching the carnage take place.

"Take her." I hear his voice but can't place it. I can't figure out how I got to this dark and dismal place.

"What do you want me to do with her?"

There's a moment of silence that makes the pounding in my head and heart stop.

"Put her in the dungeon," he orders emotionlessly. I feel my body being lifted and carried. It means nothing to me. In the end, I know what my fate will be. It will be the same as these people's.

Death.

Alzerro

Does she have a fucking death wish? My body is bursting with aggression and anger. She'll be lucky if I don't kill her tonight. I rip my suit jacket off, throwing it against the wall. How dare she try to tell me what I can and can't do!

You're more than this, Figlio... my mother's voice enters my mind. Fuck. I can't handle this…

She still shouldn't have defied me. She should have listened and kept herself quiet. Now I'm forced to teach her a lesson.

Pulling my slacks and dress shirt off, I slip into a pair of jeans and head down to the dungeon. My steps are heavy with anger, madness even. I'm not sure if I want to fuck her into submission or kill her.

I grip the key in my hand tightly, begging for the pain to release some of the anger I have within me.

Sliding the key into the door, I scrutinize her. The anger I felt moments ago dissipates. It's still there, but it has eased. She's lying on the bench seat, her dress clinging to her.

I take slow and steady steps toward her. I'm still debating if I will hurt her or not. I want to. I want to shake the hell out of her for making a fool of me in front of my men, in front of the people who owed me and my family money.

Her face is turned toward me, and it's then that I see the bruise on the side of her face. It's black and blue and against her creamy skin, a dark reminder of what I'm capable of doing.

My stomach sinks as realization dawns on me. I did this to her! Suddenly, I want to laugh. I've killed women, countless ones, ones who were mothers, daughters, aunts…it didn't matter. I ended their lives, but the mere thought of blemishing Bree's skin in any way has me sinking to the ground on my knees.

This is fucked up, and I'm fucked up for thinking such thoughts.

A cut mars her top lip, and I know if I look at other parts of her body, I will see more signs of my darkness.

Gripping my hair, I take a step back. I'm feeling conflicted; I've never in my life felt conflicted before. I always know what to do. There's never a doubt in my mind if someone deserved to die, if someone deserved pain.

A whimper leaves her lips, and I find myself kneeling down by her face before I can even stop myself. I cup her face in my hands. The blank look in her eyes and that bruise make something in me snap.

I wonder if she can be the exception to it all. She's paying a debt, though, I remind myself. I've never allowed anyone to get close to me. No one. Not since my mother. Losing her was the nail in my coffin; it closed the door to my heart.

But Bree has to pay for what she has done. It's weak of me to think this way, and to want to keep her and do things with her is not like me. I'm stronger and smarter than this; she'll not break me. I hope she learned her lesson tonight. Forcing myself from her angelic face, I stand. She'll have to pay.

Turning, I walk out, shut the door, and lock it. She'll learn that no matter how much she tries to sway me from evil or tells me that I can't do something, that I'm damned and will be this way forever.

It has been four days since I've gone and checked on Bree. I force myself to stay busy with business, but it does me no good. My mind still wanders to her…

"She's begging that we release her," Mack reports, entering my office. I don't look up from my computer.

"She was begging yesterday too." For the past four days, she has begged and pleaded to be released. I'm not sure if she thought she would get away with what she did, but this is teaching her otherwise.

"She screams and cries every time we go down there." There's a sappiness to his words, and when I finally look up, he kind of looks heartbroken.

"When did you grow a heart?" I joke. Mack is one of the most ruthless of my family friends. That's why he's still here and no one else is. In this business, you can't bless someone with mercy because if you do, they will take it and run. Plus, if you do it for one person, you have to do it for everyone.

"I didn't grow a heart. I'm just not immune to a beautiful woman's cries." The smile he shoots at me sends a rage deep within me to the surface. Does he want her too? She's mine, and I won't have any problem putting him in his place.

"Are you attracted to my debt?" I demand an answer. We won't be leaving this office until I got one.

"No, sir… I didn't mean…" I cut him off, not wanting to hear his sputtering.

"Good. Leave her be. I will go down there in a few and take care of her." Along with dealing with her and obtaining payments for debts, I have to contact Luccio and ask him if he has found anything out about my mother's killer.

I slam the laptop closed and drag myself from the office. I can hear her pleas as I draw closer to the basement. If she doesn't want to be punished, then why the hell does she act out in ways that she knows will get her punished?

I push the key into the lock and throw the door open. She has hit a nerve. My eyes land on hers, and her pleas stop immediately as her eyes widen. She moves herself to the far wall of the cell as if she's repulsed by my presence.

"I heard your pleas, and my cock came to fulfill them," I announce arrogantly, smirking at her. I take a step closer and watch her body shudder. She's afraid of me, as she should be.

"You're a sick asshole!" Her words are flung at me with such intensity, I can practically feel her anger against my skin.

"I already know all those things, sweetheart. You're not the first to say it and won't be the last." I'm being a cocky bastard because her pissed off, angry demeanor makes me want to fuck her into oblivion.

"Don't. Touch. Me," she snarls. There's a fire in her eyes, something I've never seen before. If I were a betting man, which I am, I would bet she's slightly turned on.

"You tell me not to touch you, but your body says differently…. Your body says fuck me. Long. Hard. Strokes."

I didn't come down here to fuck her, but if the situation is right…

"I want nothing to do with you. Nothing. What you did to me…to those people…" Her eyes glaze over as she relives the whole scene. I'm sorry for hurting her the way I did, but I'm not sorry I did my job. Those people had to die. She doesn't understand the business, and I'm starting to understand where her distaste comes from, but she isn't me, and she needs to understand there are rules that must be obeyed.

"Those people made a deal with me. I've explained how this works many times…" I stop myself from calling her little one. "Bree, I understand that you can't comprehend or accept any of this, and that's fine. But you had to be punished for your blatant disobedience and disrespect. My job is simple: I'm a leader. If I don't follow my own rules, then no one else will. There would be mass chaos, and more people would have to die."

I'm trying to be gentle, which is new to me. Her face lightens just a bit as if she's finally digesting what I'm saying. Her bruise is lighter, and it looks like she's using the creams I've been sending down with Mack. Even though she's being punished, I make sure she has clean clothes and food every day.

"You still killed people. People who had families, who could have been working hard to pay you off. People who come to you are in dire need. You're their only hope. Just like my father…" Tears well up in her beautiful, brown, doe eyes. My chest constricts as I take another step forward.

"I don't have to justify my…."

"You're right. You don't," she agrees, cutting me off. "But you shouldn't just go around killing people. You shouldn't kill people without knowing their struggles."

"Their struggles aren't my problem. Not everything in this world is rainbows and fucking sunshine, Bree. Sometimes life is hard; it's a bitch, and no matter how many times you hit it, it gets back up. I can guarantee that none of those people would have my back if our roles were reversed. No one out there has your back as much as you do."

She sniffles, her eyes filling with more tears, "I don't fucking care. Kill me or let me go. I refuse to stay here with you. You're a mindless, disgusting bastard who gets off on bloodshed, and that's not okay with me. I didn't sign up to be shacked up with some lunatic."

I laugh because, well, it's funny, and if she thinks I'm crazy, she should see some of the sick bastards who walk freely in the world.

"You didn't sign up for this? Well, neither did I, darling. But I can tell you that your father did sign for money, and he made a blood oath to pay it back. You're the payment, so no, you cannot go, and no, I won't be killing you. Yet. What good is money if it's dead?"

I smirk because I'm a fucking prick like that. I watch as her eyes skim the cell. There's nothing for her to throw at me. Her bed is shackled to the wall. The small toilet and sink can't be moved, and she wasn't given any sharp objects.

"Then I'll just do it myself…" She lunges forward, as if she's going to do something. Except I'm faster and more experienced when it comes to fighting. If that's what she wants, she doesn't stand a chance.

I grab her, my touch gentle. She struggles against me, her elbow coming to land against my stomach. It doesn't affect me, though. I've been shot at, punched, kicked, and beaten many-a-time.

"Stop," I demand, pushing her back onto the bed. She squirms even more, as if she thinks she can actually get away. She needs to stop—she's making me hard with every scrape of her thigh against my cock.

Since she won't stop, I decide to take matters into my own hands. I push my weight onto her, which in turn pushes my cock against her thigh. A gasp leaves her lips as her heart races under her shirt. I can hear it even without being against her chest.

"Get off of me!" she cries out. It sounds like a cross between a need and a hate. It's as if she wants me in that moment, but at the same time wants me to go away. If that is the case, I completely understand.

"I know you want it. You want me as much as I want you. You want my cock inside your tight pussy, don't you?" I push my arousal against her again, thrusting my hips in an upward motion.

She shakes her head no, but with every small thrust, she sighs as if it alleviates some of the pressure deep within.

Her eyes darken, and her tongue dips out onto her bottom lip. She wants me. I know it, and she knows it. It's getting there that is going to be the hardest part.

"Let me fuck you… Let me satisfy all those desires deep inside that pretty little head of yours." My hands caress her as I leave a kiss against her neck.

"You're demented," she hisses. She's on the edge, at the point where she wants it but she doesn't. I just need to give her that last push into wanting…

"Yes, I fucking am," I murmur against her ear as I suck it into my mouth. I hear her cry of pleasure, and I'll be damned if my heart doesn't speed up a little bit.

"This is wrong…" she utters between pants. I know why she thinks it's wrong, but I don't care. She'll have to understand and learn if she ever plans to make it in this life.

"Nothing is wrong. It's merely what you think is right and wrong that has you confused." I push her down, parting her legs with my own. Devouring her neck and ear, I wait for her to say the final words.

I may be a bastard, a ruthless killer even, but I'm not one for taking women against their wills. There's always a tight, warm pussy that wants my cock. There's no need to take when it can be given by others.

She quivers, her hips gyrating against my own. She whimpers again, her eyes opening. They shine brightly back at me as I slide my hand down to her sweatpants, cupping her there. Her head falls back, and her eyes close for a brief second.

"We can't," she states, fighting against it. I will admit she's strong, but I'm stronger.

"Then I'll taste you… I'll have you begging to ride my cock…" I murmur in her ear as I pull myself off of her. Gripping the hem of her shirt, I pull it off in one swift movement. Her pants follow suit, and she lies before me in nothing but a black thong.

"It was wrong. What you did was wrong." Her words are real, and the force of them stop me dead in my tracks.

"I never said my actions were right. In my world, that is what happens when you don't pay a debt," I whisper against her skin. She smells completely delectable, and I'm holding back from taking a bite of her.

I bend down to press my lips against hers when I hear a throat clear behind me. "Sir… You're needed upstairs. There has been a break in." Mack's voice hits my ears, but it takes a moment before what he says registers in my mind. Shit.

"I'll be right up," I respond, clearing my throat. I'm flustered, and as I look down at Bree, I see she is too. At least I'm not alone in the need for pleasure.

"I need to go up there and see what the problem is." Her eyes search mine as if she's looking for something, like a missing piece to who I am. I've seen many women look at me with that same look, but most of the time it disgusts me. Disgust isn't something I feel right now, though.

"Okay," Her voice is meek.

"Stay here. I will come for you later." Pulling myself off of her takes every ounce of my will power, and it's even worse when I come to a standing position and my cock is aching painfully in my pants while she's just lying there as if she's on the menu for dinner.

"You aren't releasing me?" Her eyes plead.

"We'll talk when I come back," I promise, walking to the door and closing it behind me. Her warm eyes are on me the whole time, and I know she's down. She's sad, broken, and confused, and leaving her here is the last thing I want to do, but in the grand scheme of things, I haven't a fucking clue as to what to do with her.

I take the stairs two at a time, and at the top, Mack greets me to give me a report.

"What happened?" I furiously demand. I'm back in mob boss mode.

"Someone jumped the fence in the back yard. The silent alarm went off," Mack explains, his eyes never leaving mine.

"To the office. I can't believe you weren't watching the fucking cameras," I grumble. There should be no reason to get me; I train these men to deal with these issues.

"We were sir, we didn't see…"

"Then you go out there and check it out. There isn't any reason to get me, unless you don't have the situation under control?" I question him, wondering if he really has the situation under control. Luccio's words ring in my ear to watch my back, to protect myself.

"Sir…" Mack tries to get in, but I turn on him. In a second, my hands are wrapping around his throat. He might be bigger than I, but I'm faster.

Leaning into his face, making sure he can hear and see every word coming from my mouth, I spit at him, "You have one job, Mack. One fucking job. If you can't do your job, then what fucking good are you to me or this family?"

I've known him a long time yet have never before seen the anger that is currently flashing in his eyes.

"If you would just fuck the bitch in the basement and then kill her, maybe your head would be where it's supposed to be." My hand clenches tighter around his throat as my patience for bullshit flies out the window.

"She's mine to do with as I please. I wasn't aware that you had a problem with her. Do you have a problem?" My eyes narrow as his face grows blue in color. I know if I don't let up soon, he'll be out. It doesn't matter how big you are, if you lose air supply, you'll be out for the count.

When he doesn't answer me, I squeeze harder, my fingers digging into his flesh. Nothing matters to me anymore, or at least that's what I keep telling myself. His eyes bulge out of his head, and I can hear his body gasping for even the tiniest shred of oxygen. The noise pulls me from my mind, and I release him. I'm a monster, a horrible person, but I'm above killing my own kind.

He sucks in a breath and then another as he stands there, the life coming back to his eyes.

"Would you have really killed me over such a pathetic question?" he asks in between breaths. I ignore his question and head straight to the security room. No one is manning the desk. Fiery rage fills me. What is the use if no one is here to fucking do as I say?

Letting it go for the time being, I focus my attention on the monitors. The cameras don't show a disturbance, but the alarm is going off which means even if the intruders aren't seen, they are still out there.

"Fuck…" I pound my fist against the table. Mack is right. She's getting under my skin. She's distracting me. Making me think crazy, fucking things. Things that I can never, nor should I ever, be thinking about.

I need to handle this on my own. Hitting myself in the head a few times, I feel as if everything is finally back into place. I head toward the backdoor and out into the darkness. I'm a hunter searching for his prey. My eyes adjust to the darkness, and my body fills with tension as I ready myself for a fight.

"Come out wherever you are…" I demand, my voice that of someone I don't even know. The wind blows, and the moon shines brightly down on me as I stare up at it. How confused and fucked up am I?

A twig snapping in the distance brings me from my thoughts, and it's then that I see the shadow of a man looming by the perimeter wall. If he thinks he's getting away, he has another thing coming.

With precise movements, quietly and stealthily, I sneak up on him. His frame is large, but from his heavy breathing, I can tell it isn't muscle he's carrying around.

The moon illuminates the sky, but not enough for me to get a good look at the guy. Crossing the short distance that stands between us, I reach out and grab his shoulder, turning him around quickly and pushing his body against the brick wall.

Reaching for my gun on reflex, I realize I forgot to grab it. I never forget to grab it. *Her.*

Ah. Fuck it. Hand to hand it is. Looking at the guy, I'm not really worried. His face is heavy, and his eyes hold a secret that I plan on getting out of him.

"Who the fuck are you?" I snarl. I'm six…five…no, about one second away from ripping his fucking face off.

"I…" he stammers. I can see the fear, feel it coming off of him. I may have even gotten a whiff of piss.

"Did you just piss your pants?" I yell in his face. Spit escapes my mouth and clings to his face. He doesn't even move to wipe it away.

A whimper escapes his lips, but that isn't good enough for me. A whimper isn't an answer.

"I'm going to ask you nicely one more time: WHO THE FUCK SENT YOU?" My words vibrate within me. My teeth clench as my body begs to unleash hell on this fucker's ass.

"I work…." Well, we're making progress - two fucking words is better than one, but it isn't the answer I want.

Grabbing him by the throat, I rip the knife from my ankle where I always keep it and press it firmly against his neck. Blood trickles from the cut, but I'm not done. I will be bathing in his blood by the end of this if he doesn't provide me with answers.

"Tell me…" I sneer, pushing the knife in with more force. His eyes widen, and his breaths become pants. He's going to have a heart attack if I don't kill him soon.

"Luccio," he says the name like it's one he knows well. I narrow my eyes at him, trying to determine if he's in fact telling the truth. Luccio was the very person to warn me… Could he be the person who set me up to begin with?

"What about him? Tell me everything or so help me fucking God, I will cut your throat open and watch you suffocate." Each word is something I mean. I don't make promises; I just do it.

"I work with him…" Tilting my head at him, I grip his throat harder. "What are you doing on my property?"

"I can't tell you…"

"Well, that's a shame then…" Taking the knife, I slide it across his throat. Blood pools from him as if he's a leaky faucet. I watch the life leave his eyes as his last breaths are nothing but gurgles. Then I bend down, place a kiss against his forehead, and go on with my way. I will find out who he worked for and what they wanted.

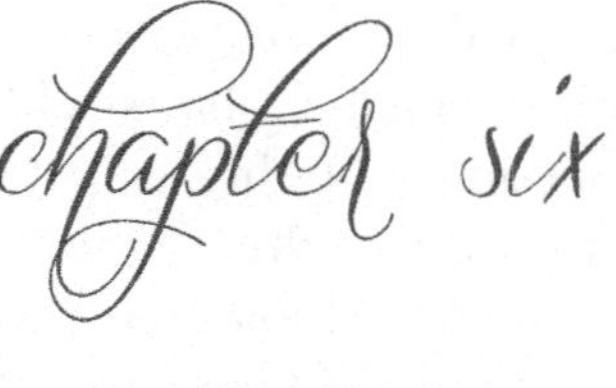

Bree

"Let me the fuck out of here!" I scream as my hands grip the bars with a ferociousness that hurts my skin. I've been locked down in this hell hole for days. The only way I can tell if it's day or night is from the tiny small window placed above my cell that has bars across it.

The only things that can be heard down here are my pointless pleas for release. Zerro said he would come back, but that was two days ago. Two fucking days I've sat down here waiting and silently hoping for him to come. Then again, at the mere mention of his name, I want to gouge his eyes out.

He causes butterflies to erupt in my stomach, but at the same time he makes me want to puke. The thought of being attracted to him, wanting him - makes me sick. How can I want such a heartless killer? It's as if God is playing a cruel game with my emotions.

Since listening to my own pleas is annoying and exasperating, I pull myself away from the bars and throw myself onto the make shift bed. There's no way out of this hell hole other than through the door that I obviously don't have a key to. Mack hasn't come down to check on me for hours, but I'm okay with that. He scares me and creeps me out. I know if given the chance, he would fuck me and then kill me without a second thought.

When he came down the time before last, his neck had purple bruises on it. He looked as if he had been choked, but I was not going to ask him about it. I don't think Zerro has it in him to kill his own kind; it doesn't seem like something he would do.

Neither does keeping me alive, but here I am. He has yet to hurt me, at least not in a purposeful physically abusive type of way. The bruise on my face isn't okay with me, but it's completely different than being beaten. He hasn't touched me, and mostly everything he does is a mind game…

I'm not afraid that a part of me wants him. It's a dark part of me, a part that craves the fear and darkness that only he can bring out in me. I'm not stupid, though. I know the path that he's on that will only lead to death. I don't want to die; I want to live. I want to be happy, go to college, get a job, and grow old with someone who loves me.

These very thoughts make me think of my mother and the days before she died. She begged me to make promises to her. They were petty, little things, but I agreed to them simply to put her mind at ease. She was already going through so much, and if making a promise made her day better and brought life back into her, I would do it.

My mind drifts to the most important promise I made. . .

"Promise me. Promise me that you'll take care of your father... He's a man, a stubborn one, but with your guidance, he can move on." Pain showed in her eyes, and I knew how hard it was for her to ask me to do something like that. She had always been the one to carry the weight, the one who made sure everything was okay.

With tears in my eyes, I promised her. "I promise, Mom. I promise to keep him in line." She smiled at me gently. I cursed God, wondering how he could take such a precious person from us. My mother must have noticed my pulling away because she spoke to me with so much love that I was shaken to the core.

"Don't fret, child. I will always be here. Right in there..." She pointed to my heart. She had given me life, had shown me the meaning of love through her relationship with my father, and I had always thought she would be here.

"When you get lost or you're worried and you don't know what choice to make, listen to your heart. I'm in there, and I'll guide you the best that I can. Remember that..."

Her words still echo in my mind as I pull myself from the sad memories. Tears form behind my eyes, and though I'm not afraid to cry because I know it doesn't mean I'm weak, I just don't want to shed any more tears right now. I don't want to cry over my mom or over the debt I'm paying in my father's name. I want to smile, be happy, and move on from all of this. Someday I will…at least I keep telling myself that. I have to deal with and survive my current situation first, but it still doesn't stop me from wondering what my mom would think.

What is my father doing right now? My heart tightens as I think of him all alone, feeling sad and guilty. Is he trying to think of a way to save me? Will Zerro let me call my dad? Let me check up on him? Will Zerro even let me go after all this? Doubts swarm me, fear owns me, and courage is the only thing driving me forward every day.

I burrow myself into my blanket as I let the doubts eat away at me. I can't run, or I will die. Zerro has threatened me, and I know that it isn't an open ended threat. Wait…

A light bulb goes off in my mind. What if I turn the gun on him? What if I take him out before he can take me out? My heartbeat skyrockets at the mere thought of shooting him. It isn't fair that he can point a gun at me and feel nothing. If it were me, I wouldn't have pointed it at him at all.

A clicking sound startles me as the door to my cell opens. Mack walks inside looking as if he would rather stab needles through his eyes than come and deal with me.

"Get up." His voice is gruff, but is full of hateful promises. I know he'll hurt me if I don't listen to him.

I stand up slowly. My body aches with all the emotions that have been swirling through me. Living in this house gives me a serious case of whiplash. Just as I steady myself, the asshole grips me by the arm, pulling me into his body.

"If it weren't for your pathetic ass, his head would be in the game." Mack wants me to hate him, to feel his anger. I can see it in his eyes and feel it in the way he grabs me. I want to bite my tongue, and I probably should, but something beyond me thinks it's a good idea to talk back.

"His head is clearly in the fucking game, asshole. He killed a room full of people while you just stood there and watched. You probably enjoyed it." I glare at him, my blood running cold.

A wicked smile pulls at his lips. It's one that causes my knees to rattle and my stomach to heave. I wish I could smack the look right off his face.

"Has he tried you out yet?" His hand travels down to my ass as he grips it harshly. I pull away from him quickly, knowing that's the last thing he expects. He'll never think of me running or fighting back.

Running through the door, I go down the hall and head for the steps that lead to the first floor. I hear his heavy footfalls behind me, and I look around in terror.

"When I get my hands on you… I'll kill you myself!" His voice sounds as if it's right on top of me. Not a moment later, the air shoves from my chest as I land against the stairs. His body is against mine, and I can feel his erection against my backside.

"Get the hell off me!" I scream. Gripping me by the arm, he twirls me around, his body pushes against mine again as he stares menacingly into my eyes. All I can think is I can't let him do this to me; I have to get away. I push against him with all my might, but my arms are pinned, and my body is exhausted.

"Give up yet?" His breath is hot against my skin, and it feels wrong. All of this is wrong, but there's nothing that I can do about it. He nips at my neck as his hand begins to slide under my pants. I shake my head back and forth, trying to make myself forget, trying to remove myself from the situation.

With the last of my strength, I scream. I scream until tears are streaming down my face, until my voice is hoarse, and he's telling me if I don't shut up that he'll gut me.

The door above us is open, so I know someone has to have heard us. Footsteps fall against the floor as I hear someone coming. Zerro's coming; he's going to save me! It's going to be okay…

An older woman peers down at us. Her face contorts into anger as she descends the steps. Her words come out in a dialect that I don't understand… It sounds Italian, but I'm not sure.

Whatever she says has Mack backing away from me. His eyes eat me, though. The way he's looking at me tells me that he'll be back to do what he wants when he gets me alone.

"Come, *Piccolo*." Her hands are gentle, and her voice soothes me. Tears spring from my eyes, and I grab her, wrapping my arms around her small frame. She's my savior, my saint.

In the haze of it all, all I can focus on is that word, the one Zerro always calls me.

"What does that mean?" I ask between sniffles. She smiles at me softly. The kind of smile my mom used to give me.

Her frail fingers reach out, pushing loose strands of my hair behind my ear. "It means 'little one' in Italian." Her voice is heavily accented, and as I listen to it, I want her to say something again. The way the words sound and come together is soothing to my shattered soul.

I look back down the stairs where I was just assaulted. Mack already left, completely enraged as he stomped off. I promise myself that when he comes for me again, I will be ready.

"Let's get you some food." My face softens as I take her hand, letting her lead me to the safety and comfort of the kitchen.

Dinner is delicious. Adaline, Addy as she likes to be called, is the head maid in the house. She has been here since long before Zerro's time, and the stories she shares with me make me forget all about the horrific things that could've taken place hours before.

Afterward, I slip upstairs, making sure I watch over my shoulder at every turn because I'm not going to be taken off guard by Mack again. I will tell Zerro whenever he gets back from wherever he went. I really, really don't want to fucking care about him or care about whatever he's doing. Except as I crawl into his bed, all I can do is see him, smell him, taste him. I feel the weight of his body on mine, his lips on my skin, and relish the passion and fire he stokes within me.

As soon as I close my eyes, I hear the front door open. Laughter and greetings sound, and then it's quiet. Footsteps follow suit, and Zerro makes his appearance. He bursts through the bedroom door. His eyes are slightly glazed, but he mostly looks tired. I hear laughter again as he turns around to talk to someone in the hall.

"Goodnight, Alassandra." His voice is velvety soft when he says her name, and I wouldn't be fucking surprised if she has her legs spread, begging for him. His voice just has that effect.

The girl says something back that I can't hear before he closes the door and turns around and sees me. Shock shows first and then something else, that same thing I saw before.

"Who let you out?" He completely ignores my presence as he takes a drink from the glass in his hand. There's no hi, hello, how the fuck are you. He doesn't even point a gun at me. To be honest, I'm kind of pissed. I so badly want to throw in his face what Mack did to me, but I don't think it will matter to him. He won't care. After all, I'm nothing to him but a payment.

"I'm not a fucking dog." I try my hardest to sound mean. I want to lash out at him with words because let's face it, I won't ever be able to physically hurt him. Mentally, though…I can do that. I can break him down, cut him, and turn him inside out just like he does to me.

"I didn't refer to you as a dog, did I?" His smirk says asshole, but his body says I-can-have-you-if-I-want-you. I hate it. I love it. I really want to shoot him.

"Where were you?" I ask, changing the subject. I know I sound like a typical housewife to be asking where he was, and since we aren't anything, I have no real reason to know. Except I want to know.

He smiles, and his eyebrow raises. I'm afraid he won't tell me since there are numerous things I know he has to be keeping from me.

"Jealously doesn't really suit you… "

"You don't know what suits me," I point out, pursing my lips

He covers the distance between us. I'm still lying in his bed, surrounded by his scent. I'm drowning in a sea of Alzerro King.

I smell the bourbon from his drink as he swirls the brown liquid in his glass. It mesmerizes me, putting me in a trance. It sloshes over the side, and eventually he brings it to his lips, drinking it. His lips lick at his drink as if he wants to get every last drop.

"I know this much, sweetheart…" He's on me, surrounding me. The monster has captured his prey. His eyes skim over my lips and up my face before meeting my gaze. "Jealously is something that you're feeling. I know it because I see it in your eyes. It's cute, in a way. There's something you must know about me, though. I don't give a rat's ass if something bothers you." He's whispering, hypnotizing me. I can't tear my eyes away from his.

"I'm the king. I do. Whatever. The. Fuck. I. Want." Every word forces his hot breath onto my face. I want to bite him just to see what he tastes like. As fucked up as all this is, I want him. I want him even when he's telling me he doesn't give a fuck about what I think.

"No. You're a prick. A self-righteous, I'll-shoot-you-at-point-blank-range prick." The air shifts around us, and my skin feels as if it's on fire.

Zerro stares at me with an expression that shows he's very much annoyed with my talking.

I open my mouth to say something, but no words ever come. The air hangs between us, and I look down to his hand around my throat, clasping it. He pushes me to the back of the headboard, and I can feel the oxygen deprivation.

"I'm not scared of you," I inform him with everything in me. Even if I'm going to die, I will do it in a fashion that is me. He'll know I died unafraid of him, and that to me is the most important thing.

A war rages within him as his muscles constrict. He can't decide if he wants to strangle me or not… He unclasps his hand, and I swallow a breath of air just in time. His hand clenches again, and I swear I feel the bones in my neck snapping.

Or maybe it's all a dream. I know the moment he makes his decision because a tenderness shows in his eyes.

"You should be…" he mumbles against my throat as he kisses the bruises that I'm sure are there. There's a tenderness in the way he caresses me. It's as if he's trying to scrub away the bad, as if he wants to take the hurt away. He's so conflicted and fucked up that I can't even find the appropriate words to describe him.

"I'm not. To be scared is showing weakness, and I know better than to show weakness in front of some self-righteous asshole." My words are laced with so much hate. I feel like I'm trying to make myself want him less, as if saying the words out loud will make him less appealing to my body and to my heart.

"Being scared doesn't make you weak…" His eyes glaze over, hazy with a memory, I'm sure. He had to have had a fucked up childhood to have turned into the beautifully damaged man he is. He never speaks of his mother or father nor does he ever mention siblings, and though he doesn't ask me about my life, he knows a lot more about me than I know about him.

"In the eyes of a monster like you it does." His lips lick over one of my bruises and trail up to my ear. The hairs on the back of my neck stand, and I feel a surge of adrenaline go through me. His teeth nibble at my lobe, and I feel myself growing weak against him. My defenses are nothing when it comes to the things he can do with his mouth.

Hot breath can be felt against my ear, but my body is long gone when it comes to talking. I want him. Despite how mean and ugly he is on the inside, my body craves him.

"You forget that every fallen angel was once an angel themselves. Monsters don't really want to be monsters. We're just like everyone else, waiting for someone to come save us from our very own damned darkness."

I pull away from him, frazzled and warm with need. Confusion is evident on my face as he looks at me, smiling. Maybe that's how he has wanted me this whole time: confused, broken, and lost with no purpose here. If I don't know anything, then I can never leave.

"Why did you tell me that?" Does he really want someone to save him? Does he even need someone to save him? Can he be saved? Can someone so dark and hateful come back from what he has done and experienced? My mind goes straight to the moment I watched him shoot those people in their heads. The light in him had diminished and left in its place is a gaping hole of nothing.

"Come with me," he growls, his eyes hungry. I don't want to go anywhere with him. My mind and body aren't on the same course, though, because I find myself standing and placing my hand in his. He leads me from the bedroom, down the stairs and into the basement.

As we descend the stairs, my mind and body clam up. Should I tell him about Mack? It occurs to me that Zerro might not believe me, that he might even accuse me of wanting and encouraging Mack's attention.

He doesn't catch my hesitation, or just doesn't care, because he continues to pull me down the stairs. The cobblestone floors are cold underneath my feet.

He pulls a set of keys from his pocket as we pass the door that leads to the dungeon that had been my home for the past several days.

The door before us is wooden, wide, and large. I wonder what is behind it, but at the same time I don't want to know. Zerro has secrets. Who knows what, or who, he has buried down here.

Opening the door, he smiles at me. It isn't a warm and friendly one, but more along of the lines of one that says I-will-eat-you-alive-and-laugh-while-doing-it.

I enter the room slowly, afraid something will jump out at any point and time. He moves behind me ever so slowly, like a snake ready to strike. The room is simple and bare, except for the drawers that line one of the wooden walls.

What they contain, I have no idea. I'm sure I'm about to find out, though.

"Go stand at the end of that wall…" He points to the far wall, the one that seems as if it's a million miles away, the one furthest from the door. How can I escape if I'm so far away?

Dread eats at my insides. Is this the end? Is he going to kill me? I try my best not to show weakness, but I know, as well as he does, that he'll kill me whenever he sees fit.

With my head held high, I walk the distance as if I'm walking to my own funeral. Turning around to face him, I stand against the wall with my back straight. If I'm going to die, I'll be dying in a way that says I stood tall and proud when I was given no other choice.

A smirk lights his face. It's devious and makes the darkness in his eyes seem that much darker. His body looks hungry for either release or bloodshed.

Silence passes, and I'm certain that this will be the end. I watch as he pulls a drawer open, his eyes growing wide with happiness as he handles whatever is in his hands.

I want to run, to escape with all my might. I want to run away from this man as much as I want to run to him.

I look up through the shitty lighting to see a big, shiny knife sitting in the palm of his hand. He grabs the end of it as if he has experience using it. He probably does…

"If you're going to kill me, just do it." The words rush from my lips before I can stop myself from provoking him. Zerro peers up at me again, pushing away a couple pieces of his dark hair that have landed against his forehead.

"I'm not going to kill you. Yet. Instead, I'm going to do something far worse…" He examines the knife as if he isn't certain that it will do its job. If he isn't going to kill me, what's he going to do?

My mind is reeling, and then in a blink of an eye, I watch him throw the knife at me. His body is so full of pent-up aggression, it's like watching a train wreck happen. He's going to kill me. I know it.

chapter seven

Alzerro

The knife lands with precision right where I expect it to— just shy of cutting her ear off. A breath of an inch closer and she would have been one ear short of two.

Her eyes are as wide as saucers. Fear is rooted deeply in them, and I know she thinks I'm going to kill her. She thinks that one of these many knives is meant for her. She's wrong. None of these knives are meant for her; they're meant for me.

"Whatever fucking, crazy ass rollercoaster you're on, I want off!" She sounds tiny, and her body is trembling with fear. I laugh in the face of it. Nothing scares me. I've lost everyone who was important to me. Being scared means you have something to lose. I have nothing.

"Sorry, no refunds, baby," I taunt, grabbing another knife from the drawer. I can go all night. There are knives upon knives that I can throw, but I have other ideas concerning what I'll do with them.

"Then kill me. Do it. Because this game, or whatever it is that you're playing, is fucking with my head. You're fucking with my head. Forget the debt, just do what you planned to do all along." She sounds like she may be pleading or begging, but she doesn't sound defeated. My dick grows harder with every heated word that passes from those full lips of hers.

Her face is flushed in fear, and I know if I remove her clothing, I'll find other parts of her flushed as well. She's beautiful even as she trembles.

"What I plan to do to you doesn't pertain to actual death, although after I bring you to the edge over and over again, I'm sure you'll be wishing that I had just killed you."

Her face shows understanding as her lips part. Is she ready for me already? Does this type of thing bring her pleasure? Maybe she's darker than I thought.

"I won't let you…" She's trying to sound strong, but I know, as does she, that if I feel between her legs, I'll find her pussy soaked with need.

"You will." I'm not full of myself. I just know when someone is lying, when they're hiding what they truly want.

She wants me. I just have to make her admit it to herself. *You want her too…* My mind is playing tricks on me. I wouldn't ever say that, feel that.

Her hair is plastered to her face, and her small legs are shaking. I slide my eyes up her legs so very slowly, taking in the slope of her thighs, imagining the way they'll feel squeezing me as I enter her.

If she feels anything close to the way she felt when I entered her with my fingers, I'm going to be in heaven. There's nothing more glorious or satisfying than entering tight, virgin pussy. My dick is rising in approval. Her pussy is mine, only mine.

I cross the distance between us, my body moving effortlessly. I still hold a knife firmly in my hand as I watch her eyes skirt to it. Fear still shows, but something else does too. Excitement? My blood stirs.

I stand directly in front of her. The edge of the knife is sharp, but I know just how to move it so that it won't hurt her beautiful skin. If she thinks she's going to die, she's wrong. I'll bring her to the edge over and over again, so by the end of the night, she'll wish I had granted her death instead.

"What are you doing with that?" Our eyes meet, her brown ones meeting mine. I smile, my eyes narrowing as I pull the knife up to her lips. A gasp leaves her mouth as she begs me with her eyes. What is it that she wants?

Pushing the knife against her full, red bottom lip, I wait for her to say something, to beg me to take her. Instead, she just stands there. I don't know if it's out of defiance or fear, but I do know it makes me want her more. I tighten my grip as I slide the tip of the knife over her skin. A small red line marks her flesh as I slide it down her neck and over her beating heart.

"Are you scared?" I whisper to her. Her breaths are hot against my skin. I'm on the verge of taking her without following through with what I want to do.

She sucks her lip into her mouth, shaking her head no. I smile sickeningly, gliding the tip from her chest back up to her collarbone. The red scratch that shows on her skin is nothing compared to what I can do to her body.

Her flimsy night shirt is no match for me. I pull it from her body, taking the knife and cutting it straight down the middle.

"Oh, God…" she murmurs softly as we both watch the material fall to the ground. She stands before me in a pair of plain white panties and a black bra. It's plain as well, but against her skin, it accents her well.

Taking the knife, I move it under the strap of her bra.

"My name's Alzerro. Please use it..." I say roughly, just on the verge of falling off the edge. I haven't even taken her panties off yet, and I'm ready to explode.

"Zerro…" she pants, her eyes wanting to meet mine. Her hands reach out, tracing across my shoulders. Her touch is soft, and my body wants it, wants her.

I slide her bra strap down and trace across her chest to release the other one. Bringing the knife back between her breasts, I push it straight down the middle, cutting the material from her body. It falls to the ground as her perfectly perky tits are unleashed.

Her skin is milky white, and her nipples are a dusky pink. I want to lick and bite at them, but I place a lingering kiss against each one instead. Her lips part as I stare at her, my tongue slipping out of my mouth and circling her nipple. She tastes sweet, like cherries and vanilla. Her unique scent surrounds me, pushing all thoughts to the back of my mind. Making her come is front and center.

I kneel down before her, scraping the knife across her skin. By the time I get to her panties, I'm panting with need.

I slide the knife across her hips, watching as her panties fall to the ground. Nothing is separating us anymore. She's spread out for me. Mine.

Her pussy is freshly shaven, and it calls to me. Her pulse jumps as I separate her lips, my finger sliding through the slick wetness. Her need for me can be seen and smelled from miles away.

"You want me?" I growl. It isn't really meant to be a question, but more like I'm letting her know that I know. She says nothing, other than allowing a gasp to leave her lips. I push her legs apart.

Gripping her behind one leg, I place it over my shoulder. I want to feast on that sweet, slick pussy.

"Please," she greets me with a begging plea as she lifts her other leg and places it over my shoulder to allow me to grip her ass and bring her pussy to my face. The knife falls to the floor. She smells delightful, and I can't decide what I want to do more—fuck her or eat her out. I nuzzle her, and I feel her legs grip my face tighter. I smile like the prick I am.

My tongue darts out, circling around her clit. "Fuck…" she cries out. Her fingers grab at my hair. Fuck is right… Nothing in this world can pull me away from her.

Leaning forward, I lick her from back to front, over and over again until her legs are shaking. Her hips move feverishly, and I can tell from the purrs she's making that she's right there.

I enter her slowly with one finger, testing just how close she is. Her muscles clench around my thick digit as I suck her clit into my mouth. Who knew such a small, little thing could bring such great pleasure?

"Yes… Yes… Fuck, yes…" She barely gets out as her pussy grinds against my face. I don't mind, though. I'm smiling, sucking and nipping at every piece of her.

She tastes just as she smells, and I pull her off of my face, making sure that I hold her body up as I remove my own clothes. From the faraway look in her eyes, I know I'm working her over so well.

"I'm going to fuck that tight pussy now, *Piccolo*." A sigh leaves her mouth as I lift her up by the ass. I stare into her hooded eyes. Parting her thighs, I position myself at her entrance. My cock is stiff with need. Dipping a finger inside of her, I take the wetness from within and rub it onto my cock.

I stroke myself hard, a hiss leaving my mouth as I press into her folds. "This is what you do to me. You make me a crazed monster…" I murmur against her flesh. My teeth bite down on her shoulder as I push into her ever so slowly. She's tighter than anything I've ever felt.

A cry escapes her lips as I release my hold on her shoulder and look into her eyes. Being a virgin, I know she's overwhelmed with emotion and pleasurable pain, so I sit still for a moment before pushing into her all the way.

No words need to be said. I plan on spelling everything out plainly and simply. My strokes and bites will be my words.

"Your pussy is mine…" I croon as I wait for her to adjust to my presence inside of her. It's all mine for the taking. I'm going to pound her so hard…

"More…" she implores, her eyes rolling into the back of her head as I pull out and slam back into her. Her ass slips from my hands, making me tighten my grip. My muscles clench, and I'm going to tear her apart if I don't slow down.

"You get what I give." I don't sound like myself as I pull out and push back into her. My cock is swelling. I feel my balls squeezing, wanting to release even though we have hardly begun.

Sweat covers our bodies as I stare at her, nose to nose. Determination shows in every push of my body into hers. It's my will to break her beyond repair, to bring her into the darkness with me, and allow her to be that one person who prevents me from destroying everyone and everything.

Her nails dig into my shoulders while her tits bounce up and down. My pace picks up, and eventually her head falls back against the wall as an obscene amount of swear words leave her mouth.

Smiling against her skin, I feel my muscles coil, telling me that my release is coming and is coming fast. A few more strokes and she'll be there, so I need to last it out.

Slipping my hand between us, I place my thumb against her clit. She cries out, her muscles clenching my dick like a vice. Her screams are hoarse, and I pull myself from her as she melts into a mass of nothing. Holding her up against the wall, my hand strokes my cock tightly.

Since the moment I brought her here, I've had the need to mark her, to make sure that she knows she's mine. My strokes become harder and faster. Every slide over my head and back up pushes me that much closer to where I want to be.

"Fuck, yeah…" Her eyes are mesmerized as she watches me. I grit my teeth as my release comes, squirting all over her beautiful stomach and thighs. I want to rub it in, but I also want to make sure every ounce of my seed lands on her.

As I continue to jerk off, she moans, her fingers sliding through my semen. She's rubbing it in for me. I'll be fucking damned if my dick doesn't want to take her again.

As she rubs it in, I stare, unable to pull my eyes from her body. She's everything I want and everything I need to stay away from. She's a weakness, and I'll only bring her down if I head down a road where I think it'll be okay to want something more from her.

Love isn't in my cards. It's hard to love someone when every person you've ever cared about has been ripped from you.

Sliding one arm under her knees and the other cradling her head, I hold her against my body. She's a tiny thing, light but curvy.

"Let's go to bed," I whisper against her skin as I watch her eyes close. She falls into a blissful sleep before my feet even hit the top steps. She's the angel, and I'm the devil. There's no saving us from the destruction I'll eventually cause.

Bree

It has been three days since I had the most mind blowing sex of my life. Zerro is a dark man, but I'm starting to crave him. He hasn't fucked me since that night, and though I've given him blow jobs and allowed him to go down on me many times, we still haven't connected again.

"Get out of bed," he orders, his voice stern. He has started to become angrier every day, and just the other night when I heard him conversing with Mack, a bottle of bourbon was smashed against the wall.

I roll my eyes at his command. He might have a hold over my body, but my mind is mine to keep. I can say whatever I want in my mind, and if I had the courage, I would say it out loud.

"Out," he orders again, coming to my side of the bed. I grunt, my feet hitting the floor. We have gone over this. I told him there will be no ordering me around, and though he didn't agree, I figured I had gotten my point across. Obviously not.

"I'm up. What the fuck crawled up your ass and died?" I stumble from the bed and toward the closet.

Grabbing a pair of jeans and a T-shirt, I walk away from him, leaving him to wallow in whatever is making him mad. He's mad all the time, grateful for nothing I'm sure.

I slip through the bathroom door, fully intent on closing it and locking it when his body slides through, stopping me.

"What do you want?" I ask, disgusted by the fact that he can't, no won't, leave me alone.

"Why did you accept the debt for your father?" His eyes hold this curiousness that bothers me. But he isn't curious. A man like him is never curious. He has a reason for asking everything that he asks.

"If you think I did this because I thought that it would be fun, you are fucking crazy…" I laugh, not the normal, hunky-dorey kind, but the kind that makes me look like I'm crazy.

Raising an eyebrow at me, he watches my facial features as if he's trying to catch me in a lie. "That's not what I meant. I mean, why would you just step up to the plate?"

"Why would you take an innocent girl and bring her into your sick and twisted life? You should apologize for the monster that you've become," I retort. Who does he think he is? Questioning me has been his plan all along. He has to know that most people who borrow money from him will never be able to pay him back. Which, in that case, means he does what he does knowing the outcome is almost always going to be death.

His face twists into an angry scowl. I don't want to push him, but then again I do. My blood sings for him to take me, to slam my back against the wall and push my panties to the side…

"Me apologize for being a monster?" he growls, stepping more and more into the bathroom, forcing me to take steps back until my back hits the vanity.

"Why should I have to apologize for the very thing that these people have made me out to be? WHY should I have to say sorry to anyone…" His face is in mine, anger is right on the surface of exploding within him.

Lifting my chin and staring him straight in the eyes I explain, "Because, people who are innocent and just trying to get by die because of you. You kill people because of a debt that is meant to be paid? Did you ever think that these people come to you as a last resort? Have you ever lost anything or anyone? Probably not… You don't even know the pain…."

His fist raises and comes down, though it never hits me. The mirror directly behind us shatters. Shards of glass go flying in every direction, and I push past him and out of the way as blood pours from his hand.

Hate, deep and ugly, radiates off of him. "I know loss, pain, and heartache. You take my mercy for kindness, but I'm not kind! I'm not soft!" he screams at me.

They say you should never look death straight in the eye, but I guess you'll say I'm a bit of a rebel. I can see the misery, anger, and insecurities within him swirling. He wants me to think that nothing can break him, that there isn't anything on the face of the earth that can bring him out of his own personal hell.

"You are, or you wouldn't have taken me instead of ending my father's life." I don't let the way he's looking at me scare me. I don't let his beautifully dark face tarnish my mind.

"You know nothing…" he spits out, his hands reaching into my hair. He tugs it hard, and my scalp burns while my walls clench. The pleasure and pain he can bring me has me wanting to set him off non-stop by looking him straight in the eyes, defying him, and pushing him.

"I do…"

His eyes look into mine, all pieces of the human I've grown to know gone. His mouth descends on mine, our teeth clash, and there's extraordinary power in that simple skin on skin contact. His hand is still in my hair, holding me in place, and I can't help but feel all over his body.

He groans, gripping my ass and lifting me up onto the counter. The glass that has broken pricks against my skin, but I don't care. Nothing can pull me away from this man. My hunger for him outweighs everything.

His lips devour mine while he bites at my skin. My legs spread all on their own as I ready for him. His hand reaches up, tearing my panties from me. The flimsy night shirt I'm wearing is no resistance to him.

I'm panting with need by the time he releases my hair and pushes me back so he can unbuckle himself. I watch as he slowly pulls his pants off, his cock coming to attention, and I feel my mouth watering. The thought of him taking me, with no intent of warning me, has me growing wetter by the second.

"Hold on. . . I'm going to fuck the defiance right out of you," he croons in my ear, his teeth grazing me, and I let a sigh escape my lips. My ass is tugged to the edge of the counter, and suddenly he's at my entrance, entering me with an intensity I've never felt in my life. Our grunts and slaps echo through the bathroom. Zerro's fingers bite into my flesh as a flutter runs through me and straight to my toes. They curl, and a cry of pleasure leaves my lips as I open my eyes and catch him watching himself push in and out of me.

"Your pussy, your body… It's all made for me," he growls, his teeth scrape my skin as his cock continues to push into me, hitting my G spot. I've never felt so much pleasure in my life. Something in me comes to life, and I feel myself floating. My body tingles and zings with desire, pleasure, and pain.

He continues his destructive pace, as if he's trying to break me into little pieces so he can put me back together as he sees fit. Reaching up, I grip his face, bringing him nose to nose with me. Desire pulls deep inside of his eyes, and suddenly we're moving as he slams my back against one of the walls. The air leaves my lungs as he places deep kisses against my neck and chest. I'm so far into a lust induced state that I don't even care what is going on. My only want and need is Zerro.

"Tight pussy and your tits, they're fucking gorgeous, just like every other aspect of you." His words are a whisper to my soul, but barely heard by my ears. His grip on my ass tightens as he moves us again, his back landing on the bed with me on top of him. His hands move from my hips and come to a still behind his head as he smirks up at me.

Looking down at him, I ask, "What are we doing?"

"Ride me. Show me what that tight pussy of yours can do. I've never had a pussy that can bring me to my knees like yours does. I want to know if you can make me beg, plead, and want more."

Gyrating my hips slowly, I smile. "Your wish is my command." I move slowly at first, watching as the smirk slowly slips from his face. His lips part, and his tongue touches his lips, licking them in anticipation. I bounce on him, until I feel myself on the verge. My walls clench as my mind slips from my body, and I feel as if I've been looking at everything wrong above me. Is it possible to die from coming so many times?

A moment later, I'm lying on my back as he parts my legs and then pushes them down into my chest so he can go deeper. His pace is evil as he slips in and out slowly, then it's as if all hell breaks loose, as if he breaks loose. He pushes into me with all his might, his dick hitting my back wall with a painfully pleasing feeling.

As soon as it starts it's ending, and I feel him coming deep inside of me. I feel his spurts of hot semen and his dick swelling as my walls clench him once again.

My body feels as if it's floating, and I've never in my life felt such great pleasure in pain.

He pulls his cock from my body, leaving me feeling as if I've lost a part of me. Just as I'm coming back down to earth, I think I hear the words, "She'll be the death of me," slip from his lips. Any thought of getting up now is lost as I slip into a deep, dark, comatose sleep.

"Wake up," Zerro mutters in my ear. I roll over, my naked body colliding with his dressed one. How long has he been lying next to me, watching me sleep?

"What time is it?" I ask sleepily. I look out the window and catch a glimpse of the setting sun. I've slept the whole day? I guess I understand now how hard it is to remove yourself from someone's bed after an intense round of sex.

"It's time for you to get up. We're going to meet someone very important to me. However, we're going to dinner first." The way the word dinner rolls off his tongue sends my body into overdrive. Is this a date? Or is it just a mafia king and his indebted eating dinner together?

Groaning, I stretch. My body is sore, in a deliciously well worked-over way. My pussy aches, and as I stand, my legs feel like jelly. I grip the side of the bed, trying to get a grip on my footing. *Come on, body, get it together.* As I get my footing, I turn to see a very amused look on Zerro's face. He's so cocky, he makes me want to punch him.

"Did I fuck the defiance out of you?" he asks, smirking. I roll my eyes as I saunter to the bathroom.

"No. Did I fuck the bad out of you?" I ask with a cheeky grin before closing the bathroom door. The mirror fragments have been picked up, and a whole new mirror sits before me. Was it all a dream? I touch the mirror, as if my fingertips can bring the dream back.

The glass is cold under my fingers, and I pull my hand back, finally catching a glimpse of my face in the mirror. I look like a five dollar whore. Fingertip markings can be found on my legs, hips, and arms, my hair desperately needs brushing, and my lips are red and chapped as if I've been kissed for hours.

I run my fingers through my hair, hissing at my sensitive scalp. The hours before swarm me - the way he had taken me, the way he had possessed my mind and body… It was all about him and me in that moment. The mafia, payments, debts, deaths…nothing mattered except for our connection. Zerro may be a lost cause to most, dark and dangerous to others, but I've never felt closer to anyone than him.

Stopping myself from thinking of the way his cock tastes in my mouth, I head to the shower, my mind turning my blissful thoughts into shit immediately. Even if the sex is good, and he hasn't killed my yet, it doesn't mean it isn't going to happen. Once I've served a purpose to him, it'll happen. I know I need to stop myself from thinking that he can be saved, but I don't think I can. I see that sliver of hope in his eyes. He still believes in himself somewhere deep inside the darkness that holds him.

I turn the water on, running my hand under it until I get it to the temperature I want. Then I slip into the shower, letting the hot water hit my skin. The bathroom smells just like him, and I find myself reaching for his body wash and smelling it. It's not a complex smell, nothing that has a fancy name to it. It simply smells clean, manly if you will.

I put some onto my hands and wash my body with it. He doesn't have any feminine bathroom products, and I'm not sure whether or not I should be happy about it. He doesn't seem like the type to have a girlfriend, but he does seem the type to use and abuse. He hasn't talked to me about his past, any exes he has, or what he does for work. All I know about him is that he's a mafia king and that he has money.

I lather the shampoo into my hair, scrubbing it in frustration to the things that are going on around me. I know nothing about him or the darkness that cloaks him, cloaks everything that he is. Mack, being the only person I can possibly go to, isn't an option. Not after what he did, or almost did, to me.

A sigh leaves my lips as I slip back under the hot stream of water. I still haven't told him about what Mack almost did, or how he has treated me. Not that I thought that it will do me any good. If Zerro can kill a whole room of people, I'm sure he can care less about a woman being raped.

I rinse away the soap, wishing to also rinse away the way I'm feeling inside. Even if there's a sliver of hope and light left in him, can I save him and walk away unscathed? Something tells me it won't be that easy.

I shiver as I shut the water off and watch it go down the drain. I'm stalling. I'm not sure what will take place tonight. I don't know that there will be anything that will occur between us.

"Five minutes," he says, tapping against the wood door of the bathroom. I pull myself from my thoughts and force myself to dry off. I need to get out of my head. There's no point in trying to hide inside my own mind.

Once my hair and body are dry, I wrap the towel around my body and slip through the door. The room is empty as I tiptoe over to the bed. A glimpse of red catches my eyes as I take in the red dress that lays on the bed. I touch the edge of the dress. The material is soft, similar to the other dress I had been given.

Who is this man? He dresses me, fucks me like he owns me, and he's dark and full of secrets. I have a decision to make. I can wear the dress or defy him and wear something else. It's beautiful, though, and I know just looking at it that it will look good on me. However, won't doing what he wants be giving myself over to him?

Then again, I've no idea where we're going, and if I don't wear the dress, he'll just make me put it on anyway. Growling, I curse him and his explicit dress choice. I pull out a pair of black panties and a red strapless bra.

I slip the dress on, relishing in the softness that envelopes me. I feel as if I'm wrapped in the softest blanket in the world. The dress is very similar to the other dress, except this one is tighter. My body curves into it like a glove. My breasts are accented very well, and my waist line looks tiny.

"You look exceptional…" His dark voice says behind me. I hadn't heard him slip into the room, and that is probably because I can't stop staring at how I look in the mirror.

"Compliments of you of course…" I say smugly, unable to wipe the look off my face. I know if I start going soft, it will be a lost cause. I have to get out of this alive.

A smile peeks at his lips… "Who else knows your body like I do?" he questions. He's trying to make my mind drift back to the time we shared this afternoon. It had been intimate and passionate. It is something I will be thinking about for many days to come.

"You don't have to buy me shit… I don't need any more debt to have to be paid…" I trail off, my fingers fidgeting with the edge of the dress. A pair of kick ass heels are next to my feet, but I'm not sure I want to wear them. I can hardly walk in flat shoes, let alone heels.

"Consider it as a gift, then." His voice is cool and suave, and his face is void of all emotions. He's dressed in black slacks with a red tie and a white shirt underneath. He dresses to please, and just looking at him makes me want to run straight to the bed and forget about doing anything. He oozes so much sex and confidence that it consumes everything in its way.

"No, thank you," I respond as nicely as possible while gritting my teeth. I kind of hate that he has all this power. He controls people, and not only other people, but now me too.

He smiles softly, which is surprising because nothing in him is soft. "Put your shoes on, please. We need to get going." Those are his last words to me before slipping his hands into his pockets and leaving the room. Those hands, the very things that cause pain and pleasure in so many ways.

He's a force to be reckoned with. I just don't know if it will be me to bring him down or himself.

chapter nine

Alzerro

"Go get her," I speak firmly to Mack. His eyes bore into mine for a moment longer than I would like before he goes upstairs to my room. Bree has found a way under my skin, and every day that she's here, I feel myself losing my grip on things. I'm not soft; I can't be. In this world, there's only strength or weakness. Being weak is certain death, and strength is power, something you need when you have men breathing down your throat and people shooting at you.

Speaking of which, I'm going to kill Luccio tonight if he doesn't give me the answers I expect. Someone sent one of his men to my home for something. That something is unknown to me, but I'm going to find out. When he and I last spoke, he seemed so intent on helping me find my mother's killer. Now it seems as if he's the enemy, just wanting to weasel his way further into my life, hoping I'll expose any and all secrets.

My fists clench with anger. Isn't that what everyone wants? Bree too? To weasel their way into what makes me tick? To break me down? I hear the faint sound of heels on the floor and avert my eyes to the stairs. The second my eyes land on Bree, I swear I want to give all the anger and madness away.

Her dress fits her just as I envisioned it would, hugging all her beautiful curves and accenting her body for what it is. Her eyes hold a secret, and I can see the fear in them. Her body is bound tightly with something, and the way she pulls away from Mack has me wondering if he has tried something on her.

She takes the steps slowly, her heels clacking along the way. I set this dinner up in an effort for us to get to know more about one another. I know all there is to know about her father, but not much about her. I know that we share heartache in the deaths of our mothers, but that is our only similarity. Bree is a college student, she's undecided in academics, and her favorite color is green. She's deathly afraid of bees, and her favorite ice cream is double fudge. My men found all of this out via the internet and other tools that aren't known to the public.

I extend my hand out to her, and she places her warm palm into mine before I lead us out to the waiting car. She looks beautiful, although I'm sure she already knows it.

"Where are we going?" she asks urgently. She seems uneasy.

"Why does it matter where we're going?" I ask, pulling the flask I keep in my jacket out. I need a drink. She's sitting right fucking next to me, and every glance at her has me imagining the way she rode me that morning. The way her hips moved, how her thighs gripped me, and her insides quivered as I….

"It matters because I'm human, and I deserve to know where you're taking me." Her voice is defensive and her nose scrunches up in anger. I smile, tipping back the flask as the bourbon warms my insides.

I screw the cap back on, my attention turning to her. I know the answer to my earlier question. She accepted her fate because she wanted to protect her father. I suppose I would do the same had I any known family members alive.

"Dinner. A nice, little restaurant in the city. I made reservations and figured you might want to get out of the house for a bit." All that I've said is true. She has been stuck in the house for weeks, and if I were her, I would've been going stir crazy. I, at least, had a chance to see my cousin, Alassandra.

"Awfully sweet of you…" She's mocking me. I know it, as does she.

"See, I'm not always a monster." Giving me a dirty look she shifts her body away from mine so she can look out the window. It doesn't matter to me that she knows where we are or how to leave the house. Where she is isn't meant to be a prison. If she runs, I will kill her, and that much she knows. Except now I'm starting to wonder if I really would pull the trigger.

The ride goes smoothly as I pull my phone out, sending Luccio a text to let him know I will be stopping by later. I will find out why he sent a pig to me. I will also inform him that he's now dead, and he can have his men get the dead body off my property.

"Are you going to kill me after all this?" Bree asks sheepishly as her eyes stay trained on the window. I hadn't really thought about it, so I don't actually have an answer to her question.

"I don't know. Probably not, unless you give me a reason to…" It's an open ended question. This is her last chance to tell me if she'll do something crazy—like run.

She rolls her beautiful, brown eyes at me, and my dick grows hard. Her defiance makes me want her that much more. *Get your head in the game…* I can't keep focusing on her; I need to be worried about whatever the fuck is going on around me.

"I just don't want to die yet. I have so much to live for. My mom died rather young, and I want to fulfill everything before that time comes." Her words cause a hole in my chest to form. She's opening up to me about her mother and her death. God, it makes me feel more like a fucking asshole for treating her like shit, for putting her through all of this. It has to be done though, softness is weakness…

"You never talk about your parents, but let me tell you it hurts to lose someone you love like that. It feels like a piece of you died with them. I miss my mom everyday…" She says all of this innocently, without knowing my story. I clench my teeth together as sweat forms on my hands. This is the part that gets me, the part where someone wants to know about my family, or what happened to them. No one close to me asks because they already know, but looking deeply into her eyes, I can tell she deserves at least a smidge of the truth.

"I know more than you think, *Piccolo…*" My words are soft as she looks at me with concern. This is the hard part about what I do: not allowing myself to get close to anyone. It's always easier if you're closed minded and shut yourself out from the world. If I make the rules then I control the outcome. With Bree, I'm starting to wonder if I can control the outcome of all of this.

"Why do you call me that?" Her voice is hushed, and there's a sense of warmth that fills my bones. She's too innocent for her own fucking good.

I reach out, placing my hand on her thigh. Her skin is warm against my hand, and I stare deeply into her eyes, "You're a little one. Or at least you remind me of one." She won't understand what I'm saying, but she's fragile, tiny in her own way. She doesn't even realize the power that she holds. I was gone the moment my eyes landed on that picture of her in her parents' run-down farmhouse.

The vehicle comes to a stop, and Jared, my driver, is out and opening the door before she can mutter another word. I take the silence as a way to gather my thoughts. So much bad, fucking shit is going to take place if I can't figure out who has set me up.

We slip from the SUV and into the Italian restaurant I made a reservation at. I have been going to Sangerio's since I was a child. I know almost everyone who has worked here, even before I was born. The legacy started with my parents and was carried onto me. We have our own private entrance and table.

"This place is beautiful…" I hear her mumble under her breath. We head to a table outside under the small light that they have hanging above us like a canopy. The moon is shining brightly as the waitress comes to take our orders. I order two of the same thing, one for her and one for me, and then give the waitress a soft smile.

"She's going to die of the need to have an orgasm…" Bree says, rolling her eyes at me. She obviously doesn't like my softness toward the waitress. That doesn't matter to me, though, because she isn't the one who will be riding my dick night after night.

"That sucks then, doesn't it?" I say, sipping from my wine glass. I'm not a wine kind of man. Bourbon is my drink of choice. It helps drown out the darkness that always wants to break free. I stare at Bree, my eyes lingering on her cleavage. How good will my dick look sliding between her perky tits?

"If you know what it's like to lose someone, then why do you kill all those people?" Bree asks, gripping her wine glass so hard I wonder if it will break. I hadn't told her anything about losing someone, although I had hinted.

"It's a job, Bree. It's what I do. This is what my family did before me. It's not as if I have a choice," I explain, irritated with her accusation. Does she think she knows me because we fucked a couple of times?

"Everyone has a choice, Alzerro. If you know what it's like to lose someone you love, then you turning around and killing all those people makes you a hypocrite." My patience snaps, and a fire builds in my veins as I reach across the table to grip her by the throat. My hold is gentle, but I squeeze just to remind her that it's I who's in control. A soft gasp escapes her pink painted lips, and her eyes grow large with fear. My insides yearn to slide my dick deep into her while she cries and begs for forgiveness.

"There's no good and evil in this world, love. It's just me, and that's something you're going to need to learn really fast. My patience for your misunderstanding is running really thin." My grip tightens ever so slightly as my tongue slides across the sensitive part of her neck.

"Kill me then…" she grits out between breaths. Her eyes are filled with lust, and I have half the mind to push this shit off the table and throw her down, push her panties to the side, and slam into her over and over again.

Instead, I smile at her sinfully. Death will be the easy way out for her. I kill people who gave me a reason to kill them. "Give me a reason to and I will." I release her as if her skin burns me and go back to my glass of wine.

"There's a special place in hell for people like you," she spits at me. Her words mean nothing to me. She hasn't a clue the type of things that are said to me when someone has a gun pointed at them.

"No, darling, you're in that hell…" Of course, the fucking waitress decides then is the perfect time to bring our food. She sits the spinach filled ravioli in front of me and then places Bree's in front of her, but not before giving her a dirty look and saying, "Here you go, bitch." I may be a fucking asshole who kills people left and right, but no one treats Bree like shit but me.

"Don't look or talk to my guests like that again, or it'll be your job," I sternly scold our server. Her eyes grow wide with fear, tears threatening to fall from her thick eyelashes, before she turns and scampers away.

"You don't have to stick up for me. I mean after all, you're the one who was just holding me by the throat," she growls, pushing the food that had been placed in front of her away. I feel myself growing feral with every word that slips from her mouth. She's mouthy, she's sinfully sweet, and she's extremely dangerous to my sanity.

I frown at her, but continue on with my meal. I won't waste my food simply because she doesn't like hers. She's not in control. I think about telling her more about my mother and father, about what happened to my mother, but I don't. I know it might make her understand me more, but I feel like if she understands me more then she won't fear me. Once the fear is gone, I have nothing to use against her.

Time passes as I finish my meal, and she sits there with her food untouched. What a waste. The server comes and removes our plates without a word. I leave the money on the table and stand, pulling Bree to her feet. She doesn't resist, but it wouldn't matter if she did. I would drag her out of here screaming if I had to.

"Get in the car," I order, opening the door to the SUV. She looks at me as if she's going to actually attempt running. "If you're even thinking about running, I'll shoot you right in the back of the head. You won't even be able to take a breath and you'll be dead." My hand reaches to my gun, hidden behind my back. Will I shoot her? I'm not sure, and the fact that I hesitate even in the slightest bit scares me. She doesn't try anything, instead groans and gets into the car. I'm walking over to my door when Jared stops me.

"Luccio's?" he asks. His accent is very strong. A bleak look crosses his dark face.

"Yeah. Go in the back way," I answer, opening the door so I can slide into my seat.

"I don't want to fucking go anywhere with you!" she yells. She's angry, and that's fine. It doesn't change things, though.

"Thanks for telling me, but I don't give a shit what you want. The moment you agreed to accept your father's debt is the moment that anything you had to say stopped mattering. Now all that matters is how tight that pussy can clench my cock…" Leaning into her body, so our faces are almost touching, I finish saying, "Nothing that you want matters."

Her eyes narrow, the brown seeping right out of them. She looks as if she's about ready to kill me, and I don't blame her. Jared starts driving, and I watch her carefully, wondering what her next move is going to be. Someone like her can't handle this type of thing. I know when she breaks it's going to be mad chaos.

In less than twenty minutes, we arrive at Luccio's. His house is just as large as mine, and I wait for him to let us through the gate. Anger surges through me, and I let the old me sit in the back of my mind. This is business. The car starts moving again, and then we're through the gate. Looking out the window, I watch as we pass the rose garden and the waterfall.

The car comes to a stop in front of the house, and I grip the door handle firmly, turning to Bree. Her eyes are full of mystery, and I can't really tell what she's thinking about. "Keep those beautiful lips shut, or…"

"Or you'll kill me? Tie a brick to my ankle and throw me in the ocean?" she mocks, eyebrow raised.

Smiling, I say, "No. I'll fuck you to death." I slip from the car and head to her side to open the door and help her out. She takes my hand as I offer it to her. Her feet hit the ground, and she takes a brief look around.

"Alzerro…" I hear my name being said as I direct Bree to where I want her.

"Luccio," I greet him in return. He smiles, his eyes eating up and down Bree's body. Something inside me breaks. I've never been the type to be jealous, and even though she's only a debt being paid, I feel possessive of her. I feel like she's mine.

"What is the occasion?" he asks amused, not showing any worry. He should be, though. He should be scared shitless right now. I'm like the monster who hides under your bed, waiting until the moment your breathing evens out and your eyes close to attack. Little does he know he unleashed the monster all on his own.

"Just business. I would like to have a word with you." His eyes glance back to Bree, and I know he's wondering what the fuck she's doing here. That's not his problem, though.

"What about her?"

"What about her?" I retort.

His eyes narrow at my attempt at humor. "Does she know?" I watch as Bree looks between us both, completely confused and utterly lost as to what is about to take place.

"Leave her be. Let's go, Bree." My hand lands on the small of her back as I lead her into Luccio's home. The walls are littered with family photos that go back many generations. His house oozes that I-have-money-and-you-know-it atmosphere. Marble flooring with gold rivets in it make up the ground that we walk on. We pass through the foyer and head to the first door on the left. It's his office just as I know it will be. The door opens and closes behind us quietly as I guide Bree to a seat.

"I haven't gathered any new information, Zerro. I told you if I found anything else out, I would contact you." I smile smugly at his comment. The knife on my ankle feels heavy as does the gun at my back. Heavy with the need to release bullets in this lying fucker's ass.

"That's not why I'm here, actually. See, a very fat and short man came to my house. Unwanted of course. You know how I get about people who trespass, right?" I watch the blood drain from his face, and I know he had something to do with it. Someone such as him can't hide from me.

He's out for something, and I want to know what he's out for.

"It wasn't me," he immediately claims. My attention slides from him to Bree, who is sitting in one of the chairs. She looks clueless to the whole situation.

"Really? Because the moment before I slit his throat and watched him bleed out, he told me that he was a member of your group…" I say, looming over him. He's sitting behind his desk, attempting to look dumbfounded. It isn't working, though. I'm not a dumb man, and I won't be made to look like one either.

I reach down and pull the knife out. He has about five minutes before I slit his throat open. "Talk…." I growl pointing the knife at him. I know he thinks I won't do it, that I don't have the balls to kill someone I've known the better part of my life. He helped raise me when I lost all of my family, so it really is sad that I have to be pointing a knife at him at all. But lies are piling up, and in the end, you have to protect yourself above all else.

"He… He was sent to see about her…" His eyes move to Bree's, and her mouth gapes open as if in shock. I'm not much further behind her. I'm a bit shaken up as to what that man would've wanted with Bree. No one knew that I had taken her except her father, but I don't expect him to be doing much talking. After all the problems he caused, I assume he'll stay on the back burner for a while. Maybe I'm wrong?

"What did he want with her?" I ask, dangerously close to putting the blade of this knife in his forehead. There's a pregnant pause, and I grow angrier as time stands still. These people have no need to know why I have her, what I'm doing with her, or who she is. Coming around the desk, I slip behind his chair, my hand gripping at his mop of hair, pulling him back and placing the knife blade at his neck. His eyes peer into mine.

"I won't ask again. What the fuck did he want with her?" I hear Bree's gasp as if she didn't realize that I could do such a thing as put a knife to a man's throat, but I ignore it—her.

"He…" His voice stops, his heart rate increases, and my need to cut out his fucking larynx grows stronger.

"He's your guy, Luccio, which means you're responsible for him. Now answer me before I kill you, because believe me, I've given you far more time to answer than I have anyone else."

"He… There's a rumor… I don't know what it is… There's just this rumor…" His words circle over and over again as he repeats the same thing. A rumor? There's always some type of drama in the industry. I mean, we're criminals after all.

"What kind of rumor?" I ask, pressing the blade into his neck. Blood seeps slowly from a thin line I cut across his throat.

"I…." he sputters like he's going to shit or piss himself. I won't be surprised if both things take place. Still holding the knife against his throat, I release his hair and grab the gun from behind my back, aiming it at the side of his head. If he didn't think I was serious before, he will now.

"Now what kind of rumor are we talking about?"

"He doesn't have to die, Zerro. It's probably nothing…" Bree's voice is soft and slightly soothing to the raging inferno that is creeping within me.

I look up at her, my eyes growing dark. "He does have to die. When I ask a question, he is to answer. If he doesn't, he dies. Loose ends get me nowhere. If someone doesn't have the answers I need, they become useless."

"They think she's with someone," he blurts out as my eyes still linger on Bree's.

"What do you mean I'm with someone?" Bree shoots back. I hold her gaze, my eyes narrowing. Is she with someone? I never asked if she had a steady boyfriend. Jealously burns inside of me, and I would be lying if I say it doesn't hurt like a fucking bitch.

"I ask the fucking questions," I growl at her. My attention turns back to Luccio who is shaking in his boots. He's a pussy. He's supposed to be this big guy who knows all these people, who can kill anyone. It's all a lie, obviously. His men aren't even in the room with him. He's a fake.

"I mean… Not with someone. She's a pig. They think she is anyway." His words are coming out a little easier, meaning I'm losing my effect.

Bree's face is full of placid rage. "A Pig? Like someone who will squeal? I didn't even know about any of this until I was forced to go stay with him…" Her voice cuts off as I shoot her a look that says shut those fucking lips before I shut them myself.

"Who told you that? Who's working for you, or are you working for someone?"

He shakes his head. "I'm not working for anyone. I work for no one. It was just told to me from one of my men that there's someone working in connection with the FBI."

Fuck. Fuck. Fuck. FBI is serious shit. I mean the shit I do is serious, and I'm not afraid of anyone, but if an FBI agent got in among us, we would be screwed.

"Tell me which man it was." I'm no longer going to be patient. People will start fucking falling over dead left and right if I don't get answers soon.

He laughs gruffly. "The one you fucking killed." Releasing him with a shove, I walk away. I'm angry—no, I'm livid. I need him. I need to know who the pig is, if there's even one. Now I have no connections because I acted too soon. Fuck. *It's her fault…* My mind is playing games on me. I know it isn't her fault, but I still want to take my rage out on her.

"You killed another person?" She acts as if she was in shock, but at the same time wants to scold me for my ill-mannered behavior, like I'm anything but this fucking monster.

"Yes. I did," I hiss, and I'll fucking kill many more, sweetheart. Don't get your panties in a bunch." I'm being crude, and I'm slightly annoyed with her behavior.

"You're digging yourself deeper and deeper," she murmurs under her breath. She isn't afraid of me or at least not in the moment. Moving from my position, I go to sit on the stool near the window. The FBI could be on our asses, and I need to figure out who squealed. My mind is racing. I could kill them both. Time stands still as I stare deeply into Bree's eyes. Can I really bring myself to put a bullet in her head? To never see her body flush with desire? To never see her beautiful brown eyes full of anger and hate?

Running a hand through my hair, I pick up the gun and point it at her. Her eyes don't close nor does she cry out or scream. It's as if she isn't afraid at all.

"Who are you with?" I demand.

Her eyes narrow as she leans into my face, her arms leaning on the side of the chair. "If I was with someone, I already would've already had them get me out of this fucking place." I blow out a breath. I need to clear my head. For once in my life, I can't just start killing people. I need to get answers.

"Let's go…" I order, grabbing her arm. She stands abruptly, and I reach out with both hands to steady her. Her body collides with mine, and as I'm evening her out, I hear the cocking of a gun behind me. I turn just in time to see Luccio pointing the gun straight at us.

Fear courses through me for the first time as I look into Bree's eyes. She could die. I could die, though I know it will happen someday. But she, she can't die.

"You aren't fucking going anywhere. You come into my house, talking all this shit, thinking that you know all there is to know. I sent that man to you for a reason…"

I turn on him, placing my body directly in front of Bree's. Not a word passes her lips thankfully. There will be no talking yourself out of what we're about to get into.

"You sent him to lure me out, didn't you?" It isn't really a question. I now know the answer.

"Lure you wasn't really what I wanted to do… I do know who killed your mom." His voice is full of hate, as if he had a reason to hate me. I haven't hurt the man since this very day.

"Who was it, then?" I ask, pushing Bree closer to the door. Her steps are small and uncertain. I can feel the fear rolling off of her. She thinks we're going to die. And we will, unless I get a grip on this shit. My gun is still in my hand, but it's all about who can get the first shot in.

"The FBI is onto you, Alzerro. Every move you make puts you closer to getting caught. They came for you that day. They killed your mother, and they were fully intent on taking you… I got my hands on you first, though…" My mind is reeling as I place everything in a timeline in my mind.

"What are you saying?" I ask between clenched teeth. My hands are shaking with anger as I raise the gun and point it at him. He doesn't cower in fear. I don't expect him to. He'll die with dignity.

"I'm saying the FBI killed your mother, and we took you as our own before you could be taken by them. You've made us millions of dollars. My family is very grateful for all that you've done… But now… Now you're becoming more of an inconvenience to our family. You're powerful—too powerful. In this case, you must die."

The words slip from his mouth as everything registers within me. It's as if everything is playing in slow motion. I pull the trigger the same time he does. My bullet aimed directly at his chest; his bullet aimed directly at me.

My shot lands exactly where I hoped it would. Directly in his heart as I watch him slip to the ground. My body is full of adrenaline, so it takes a moment to realize that his bullet hit me in the shoulder. My skin burns, my muscles ache, and my body feels heavy. This isn't the first time I've been shot, and won't be the last, I'm sure.

I can hear Bree's screams as her arms lock onto me. She turns me to face her as a coldness sweeps over me.

"We need to go," I say quietly, pushing her back.

"You're fucking crazy! You just killed someone! And…he shot you! He fucking shot you!" She's losing it, and I need her to stay with me. I need her to stay calm because she'll be the one thing to help us get out of here.

A crazed look crosses her face as she helps me stand. "We need to leave. Now. Once his men come in and find him dead, they will come for us." My shoulder burns like a motherfucker as we make our way to the door. It's too late, though. The doors in front of us push open, and I pull myself from Bree's side and push her behind me, shooting the two men before us directly in their chests before they can even raise their guns. They are so young. Their blood seeping onto the gold flaked marble reminds me that it doesn't matter how many nice things you have because in the end, none of it matters if you're not alive. I need to stay the fuck alive.

I pull my phone out, handing the gun to Bree as I pull her along and out down the hall. The rest of his men will be on alert. They will come. I know it.

I push Jared's contact name, and the phone starts ringing.

"Sir."

"We need to leave. We're on our way out. I will meet you by the road," I huff out as we push down the hall.

"What happened?" he asks. He knows better than to not assume that something has happened. Maybe it's the way I sound, or the fact that usually when things like this happen, it isn't good. I don't know what sends him to believe what he did.

"I'm shot. I need you to contact Mack and let him know. Then I need you to take us to the cabin."

"The cabin?" He knows what the cabin is. It's our hideout. It's to be used for emergencies only. This, I think, will qualify as a fucking emergency.

"Yes, the cabin. We need to go into hiding. I just killed Luccio." As soon as I say it, I hang up, not wanting to waste any more time rambling on.

"Are you going to be okay? You're bleeding a lot," Bree observes anxiously. She's pulling me along, and as soon as we make it to the front door, I know shit is about to get bad.

"Where are you going?" A man barks behind us. He's bald and heavy set, but it isn't the fat kind. It's the fuck-you-the-fuck-up kind. I'm in no shape to be beating the shit out of this guy. We need to run.

"He's going to kill us, he's going to kill us…" Bree keeps chanting as we move down the front steps. I can hear the man's feet pounding across the ground.

"What the fuck are you doing?" the voice growls. We're moving faster, barely, but we are steadily crossing the pavement outside.

"Stop now or we'll shoot!" the muscled man yells. I don't turn around to shoot. We're outnumbered. I don't want Bree to get shot, but we need to get out of their line of fire if we have a chance at surviving this. The bullets start coming, raining down on us fiercely.

"He killed Luccio!" someone yells behind us, and I can hear them running toward us. Bree is breathing heavily as she helps carry my weight.

"We're going to die," she mutters, crazed, as we run into the bushes. We have to climb the wall, and I'm not sure I'm going to make it. I'm a tough son of a bitch, but there are bullets whizzing past us at every fucking angle. If I have to make a choice between Bree and me, it will be her. She'll get over that fucking wall if I have anything to say about it.

"They're over here!" a voice yells as the branches poke at my shoulder. I'm burning up, and my body fucking burns like I'm being eaten by the fucking sun.

"Go..." I instruct her, bending down and grabbing her leg so I can lift her up and over. She hesitates only a moment as I watch her hand reach up and grip the wall. The men are descending on us quickly, as one of the bullets comes shooting through the bush and lands mere inches from my face.

"Come on!" she screams over the bullets, her small hand showing just over the edge of the wall. My eyes are blurring as I push forward, my hand landing in hers. Reaching up with my shot arm, I grip the side of the wall to pull myself up.

"Come on, Zerro…" I can hear the panic in her voice as I push myself up. It's a slow movement, and I feel as if I would rather rip my fucking arm off than continue doing this. Just as I'm about half way over, a hand grips my foot.

"Oh no, you don't. You're going to pay for what you did…" I look down to see the asshole who had been barking at us as we ran from the house. He has a gun pointed directly at my back, as his hand on my foot pulls me downward.

It's now or never. If I don't make the selfless decision to let go of her hand, then he'll find her and she'll die too. I don't care about anything in my life, but I've grown to care for her slowly. Even a smidge of pain or hurt to her body will push me over the edge.

My hand is slipping from hers as the man pulls me down… "You'll pay. We'll torture the fuck out of you. Rip that tongue of yours out, beat the shit out of you, and then…" Silence. I hear the sound of the gun being shot but am not sure if it's his gun or someone else's.

I turn around to see the man lying on the ground, a pool of blood already starting to form around him. Then I look back up and see Bree at the edge of the wall, her small body shaking. The gun is in her hand, and she is scared shitless.

I don't say anything to her, but I'm fucking proud. I'm more than proud. I'm now the one indebted to her. The second she has me over the wall, my body goes limp. I know Jared will come. I just need to hold out a little longer. It doesn't last, though. My mind slips from my body, and suddenly everything goes black. I hope to fucking God I'm not dying. I need to tell Bree how fucking hot it is that she shot a gun.

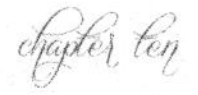

Bree

"Is he going to be okay?" I implore, asking Jared over and over again as I look at Zerro's lifeless body. He has been a douchenugget of all kinds of sorts, but I don't want him to fucking die. My body is still shaking; I'm scared to death. Never in my life have I been shot at until I met him. I have only shot a gun a couple times with my dad. He wanted me to know how to shoot in case someone ever attacked me. I don't think this was his idea of an attack.

"He'll be fine. We need to get to the cabin before I can remove the bullet, so he can heal." Jared is acting as if I haven't just told him Zerro has been shot.

"You're acting as if we weren't almost killed. This is fucking crazy." The gun is still in my hand since I'm afraid to let it go. It's the one thing that is keeping me sane and alive.

My gaze lands back on Zerro. Blood seeps into his white shirt, and his blood red tie is ripped and tattered as is my dress. The shoes he had gotten me are long gone in the rush to jump the wall. His face, though covered in a sheen of sweat and dirt, still looks as dashing as the first time I met him. I hate him for everything that he has done, for the person he is, but I also kind of care about him. I knew what he was doing when I felt his fingers slipping from my hand at the wall. He was going to save me, and even though when he wakes up, he won't ever admit it, I know it in my heart.

"What happened back there?" Jared asks me, turning down the radio. The men will be after us. I'm surprised we even made it out of there. I want to tell Jared, but the truth is, I don't really know what they were talking about, who the pig is, or what is going on. I know that Luccio was a bad man and that the FBI killed Zerro's mother and came for him. I don't know what I have to do with it, though.

"I don't really know. There was some talk about someone being a pig, and Luccio accused me of being one. Then he told Zerro that the FBI is onto him, and that they will take him out if he isn't careful. He told Zerro who killed his mother." I'm rambling because I'm scared and nervous. Will I ever be safe again? Will I be able to go back to school? Back to my dad?

"Whoa, slow down…" Jared says, trying to soothe me. His eyes shine brightly at me through the rearview mirror, and after everything that happened, I wonder if he can be trusted. Can anyone who Zerro works with be trusted? What kind of sick and twisted game is this? If Luccio was supposed to be family to Zerro and had betrayed him like that, what could anyone else do?

The gun is still in my hands, and I will use it if need be. I can save Zerro and myself from all of these people. I eye it, wondering what I should do next. Zerro must've trusted Jared at least a little bit if he called him over anyone else.

"Put the gun down, Bree. I know that look. You're scared, and that's okay. I'm not going to hurt you guys. Zerro is my friend. I'm his driver. I'm taking you to the safe house." He's speaking calmly, and I stare at him and then look down at Zerro. He's still breathing, his chest moving up and down, and I know that if I want to save his life, I need to have Jared get us where we need to be.

"Fine," I reply after hesitating a moment. I put the gun down on my lap, making sure I can grab it if need be.

"Now what happened?"

"They wanted to kill him," I huff out, my head landing on the head rest. My eyes and skin hurt so badly. My head is pounding from all the noise, and my body aches as if I've run up a hill fighting a bear.

"Kill him? Why?" he probes, profoundly dumbfounded.

I blow out a breath and take a deep one in, trying to calm myself. My stomach is still in knots, and no matter how many times I look over at Zerro, I can't help but wonder if he's going to make it. I know it's only a shoulder wound, but people have died from less serious injuries. Getting shot isn't to be fucked with.

"They said he was dangerous, too powerful, and out of control. They think I'm working with the FBI or something." I sound just as Luccio did, and I understand the look on Jared's face as he absorbs what I've said. I had that same look on my face as Luccio told me.

I watch cautiously as his hands grip the steering wheel harder. "Zerro's dangerous, Bree. I know I don't have to tell you that; I know you've seen him at his worst. However, he's not out of control. He's doing what he's meant to do in life. Luccio wanted him dead for an entirely different reason, I'm sure."

I hear his words, but they mean nothing to me. The pure fact that Luccio wanted Zerro dead is enough for me to gather that I ended up in the middle of something that is sure to kill all of us. Hell, Zerro is already on the verge of death. Even I am. Being shot at isn't something I plan on doing daily.

"It doesn't matter because now Luccio is dead, and all of his men are going to come for us. Plus, there's some fucking FBI agent, or pig, in on all of this." My voice is growing louder and louder. I'm scared and panicking. Where do we go from here?

"Just calm down. When Zerro wakes up, I'll get the full story. You're in shock, so just breathe and try to calm down." My eyes grow wide. Is he fucking insane? Somewhere in my mind I know I need to listen to him, but I just shot a gun. I just killed someone. I fucking killed someone!

"I killed someone!" I cry out as if I'm admitting my deepest sin. The gun slips from my lap and to the ground. I've seen death, my mother had died at the hands of cancer, but I've never killed someone. I feel the worst kind of hatred eating away at who I am.

"You had to. It was you or them." Jared doesn't sound remorseful at all.

"That's not me, though! I wouldn't ever kill someone. I don't even know who I am anymore...." The last part isn't meant to come out of my mouth, but I can't believe what I've done. I knew that the moment I pulled the trigger, that man would die, but I feel like I did too.

"It was either you or him. I can promise you that he wouldn't have felt anything if he shot and killed you or Zerro. He deserved it." My body trembles. Shouldn't I be crying? Am I really in shock?

"That doesn't matter. I killed someone. I took a man away from his family, a father..." The words are tumbling out of my mouth.

"You had to." The way Jared says it makes it seem final. His stare is gentle, and I know he understands what I'm going through. When I said I would pay my father's debt, I didn't think I would actually be doing this.

"Where are we going?" I ask, my eyes going back to Zerro. He's still breathing, but his body isn't moving. When I touch his skin, it's hot to the touch. I keep my hand against his hot skin to remind myself that he's still here with me. Hot skin is better than cold, right?

"The safe house is up in the mountains. It's about another thirty minute drive. Then we have to get the code for the security system from Zerro, and we can get in the house." His eyes go from me, to the road, and back again. I wonder if he thinks I'm going to shoot myself or something. I didn't survive that to end my own life.

"Why are you looking at me like that?" I ask, unable to stop myself. A smile pulls at his lips, and I wonder what he thinks is so funny. My body is still shaking, my hands sweating, my breaths still harsh… I don't find any of this fucking funny. Plus, Zerro is bleeding out next to me.

"Zerro clearly has his hands full with you. You don't seem like his type, by the way." He says it all matter of fact like. I know I'm not Zerro's type. He went for the submissive, I'll-let-you-fuck-me-however-you-want type.

"By type, you mean he doesn't usually go for the women who do whatever the fuck they want?" I ask, eyebrow raised. Jared laughs gruffly, and the tension inside the SUV eases. I'm still scared shitless, but my blood stops pounding in my ears.

"By type I mean he generally doesn't have a woman who I can judge as his type. He doesn't usually keep anyone longer than a night."

"Fantastic. I'm going to end up going to jail with the mafia king who also is a manwhore, which I already kind of assumed." Leaning over, I run a hand through my hair. My curls are everywhere, I'm sure, and I don't even want to catch a glimpse of my face.

Laughing softly he says, "Just try and relax. Once we get where we need to be, I'll let you know." I nod and return to my thoughts. All sound is non-existent in the SUV except for Zerro's soft breathing and a small amount of radio noise.

I watch out the window, afraid if I close my eyes that I will relive the scene over and over again. I killed someone. I fucking ripped him from his family and friends without even knowing it. I know nothing about him, and yet I put a bullet in his head, ending his life.

I don't even know who I am anymore. I don't know why, when Zerro's hand was slipping from mine, that it hit me. That maybe, just maybe, me being around has gotten to him. It's as if in that split second, we had reversed roles. I know for a fact that if I would have let his hand slip from mine, he would have been gone, dead to the world. As much as I wanted that to happen, a part of me couldn't let it happen.

So I pulled the trigger. I shot the man who was trying to end his life. I saved Zerro. He doesn't realize it yet, but he saved me too.

"Get some towels and water," Jared orders from the bedroom. I'm in the kitchen pacing like a maniac. He's just going to take the bullet out, clean it like a God damn scraped knee, and stich it up. Something about that doesn't sit well with me.

Filling a small bucket with water, I bring it to him. Zerro is just starting to come around.

"Get this fucking bullet out," he growls at Jared. He's thrashing back and forth on the bed as Jared uses a pair of tweezers to dig around in his shoulder. A hiss leaves his lips as his eyes seek mine out.

"Whiskey…" Jared states, pulling me from Zerro.

"Whiskey?" He didn't ask for whiskey, did he?

"Yeah, I need it to clean the wound." I get up, running to the kitchen again. I have no idea where the whiskey is kept here, if it has anything to do with Zerro, it's probably all drank.

I search the many cabinets that line the kitchen walls only finding plates, food, and silverware. I pull on a small drawer only to discover it's filled with guns. Then it clicks. Maybe he has some at the small bar in the dining room that I noticed earlier. Closing the drawer, I run to the dining room, my feet slipping on the wood floors. My eyes search the small bar shelf from a distance. BINGO. My eyes land on the bottle of whiskey.

Hurrying back to the room, I hand the bottle to Jared. "Took you long enough..." Zerro almost screams at me. His eyes are soft yet traumatized, and I understand his words aren't meant to be mean. He's in pain.

"This is going to hurt..." Jared mumbles and then pours a liberal amount onto the wound, his hands, and tweezers. Zerro lets out a loud scream and a large amount of curse words follow. Sweat forms on his brow as he clenches his teeth. I watch as Jared digs around in his shoulder some more.

Zerro doesn't move or make any more sounds. His face is full of agony, and I feel badly for him. Yes, I feel badly for him. I've watched this man shoot and kill people. I've felt his hands around my throat, and yet looking at him now, I feel nothing but pain for him. I know, deep inside, that my reaction stems from more than just a sense of compassion.

Three minutes later, Jared pulls away from Zerro smiling. "Got it. Strong fucking little slugger," he announces, dropping the bullet into a pan I brought him.

"Thank fucking God. I was about to get my gun out and shoot myself in the other shoulder," Zerro mocks. I smile at him as he attempts to sit up.

"No way. Don't move the fuck around. I need to get you sewed up. You're lucky that it didn't hit anything important," Jared orders, moving back over to Zerro. I get up from the bed, not sure what I should be doing. I'm stuck here as much as Zerro is. Not that the safe house is bad. We have internet access, television, food, and other necessities.

It's actually a cozy little cabin. Except knowing why we're here is what makes it seem like my own personal jail cell.

"Come hold him down!" Jared yells to me. I move to the side of the bed slowly. I'm not sure where Zerro and I stand after everything. I saved his life, and he saved mine. I'm sure the debt had been paid now.

Sitting down on the soft comforter, I ask Jared, "Where do you need me?"

"Just hold his arm on that side. Zerro, quit fucking moving. This isn't your first rodeo."

"Yeah, well, the first fucking rodeo didn't hurt as badly."

My mouth gapes open. I know he's a mafia man, king, whatever you want to refer to him as, but I didn't know he had actually been shot more than once.

Placing my arms against his skin, I hold him securely.

"You've been shot before?" I enquire, my face only millimeters from his. His brown eyes warm as they pass over my face and then down to my lips. I know what he's thinking. He wants to kiss me, devour me until there's nothing left of me. I know it because that's how I'm feeling.

"Yeah. I was shot in the leg when I was seventeen. Drug deal gone wrong." The way he refers to it makes it seem so nonchalant.

"Yeah and I saved his ass then too…" Jared cuts in, sliding the needle and thread through his skin.

"You didn't save me, fucker, you just patched me up," Zerro gripes as if thinking of someone else saving him doesn't sit well with him. If that's the case, things between him and I aren't going to go well. I won't rub it in his face that I saved his life, but if he tells me he can't let me go, I will remind him that he's standing here because of me. That is if I can even walk away from him.

"Shut up and stop moving," Jared shoots back, and Zerro's face turns to mine once again. I get the feeling that Jared and Zerro go way back. Not that Jared told me a lot about himself on the ride here. Aside from the small questions he had asked me, I know nothing about him.

"Are you okay?" Zerro asks, his voice is as smooth as butter. His hand that I'm pressing against his abdomen strokes across my skin. My insides turn to mush, and though I'm a mess… I still want him. He has that effect on people.

"Yeah, I'm fine…" I barely get out without a moan. I don't want to make Jared uncomfortable, and I don't really think that Zerro will be up for sex, so I just keep it to myself.

"Are you sure?" He's pushing his physical pain to the back burner. Why is he so concerned with me? Worry marks form on his face as he frowns at me. He thinks I'm lying. I really am okay. I'm shaken up a bit, and I'll forever feel guilty for ripping someone from his family, but I'll move on. I have to.

"I'm…. I'm okay. Really." I answer, smiling at him. This is something I haven't ever seen in him. I've never seen him be gentle or kind. He's always dark and crude. It's as if a switch flipped within him. Before Zerro can say anything else, Jared interrupts.

"You're good to go, King. No rowdiness." He picks up the buckets and towels and walks out of the room, closing the door behind him. Is it that obvious that we need a moment alone?

Silence passes between us as Zerro stares at me. I can't read him. I used to be able to tell what he was thinking or at least what kind of mood he was in.

"You saved my life," he states softly, pulling me down toward his lips.

"Yeah, I did. Does that mean the debt is paid?" My own feelings are starting to come forward. If he tells me I can leave, will I? Will I ever be safe without him or am I as damned as much as he is?

Anger flutters just under the surface. His mocha colored eyes turn dark as his hand reaches up into the back of my hair, holding it tightly, holding me tightly.

The sting of pain as my hair pulls makes me smile. "That debt is never going to be settled, *Piccolo*."

The smile is wiped from my face as dread settles deep into my bones. It has to be settled! We have to be even now. I saved his life!

"Why?" I cry out as he pulls me closer to his mouth. His hot breath is against my face, and he smells like bourbon and man. Sweat still lines his brow, and blood seeps through the bandage on his shoulder.

"Because now it's I who is indebted to you…" It dawns on me that he hasn't said that I still owe him. I'm just about to pull away when his lips crash against mine. The kiss is full of passion, hate, and anger. He holds me in place as I softly paw at his chest. His teeth nip at me in a way that has me parting my own lips.

"You were impossibly fucking hot when you shot that gun," he purrs against my lips. I smile, not sure what all this means. Does this mean that he owes me? That I can leave?

"I'm glad you think it's hot, but I feel really bad about killing that man. Even if he was going to kill us…" Sadness forms on my face and can be heard in my voice. I don't want to hide the fact that it bothers me that I killed someone. Zerro knows how I feel about death, about taking someone else's life. It isn't fair.

"It was you or him. I'm certain he wouldn't have given a shit about you if you died," Zerro says as if he's angry that I feel badly.

"That's what Jared said too. I know that man wouldn't have felt badly, and I know that if I didn't kill him, you would have died, but it doesn't make what I did any easier." Tears prick behind my eyes. I don't want to cry. I haven't cried through this whole thing, so I don't know why I feel the need to do so now.

"Sometimes you have to pull the trigger, *Piccolo*. Sometimes it's not about you and them as people. Instead, it's about survival. You kill or be killed, love. That's how this works." His voice is so soft it feels as though he's wrapping me in a blanket of kindness. I feel myself leaning down to lie on him, my head on his chest. We have never done such a thing, performed such an intimate act.

Kill or be killed. That's his motto.

"If you're indebted to me, what does that mean you owe me?" I ask quietly as I place a soft kiss against his chest. His muscles constrict, and I run a finger over the dips.

"It means I owe you your freedom. You're free to go whenever you want. Your father's debt has been paid in full." The way he says it makes it seem as though he doesn't want it to be true.

"What if I don't want my freedom?"

"Then you'll be mine," he growls, moving me so he can see my face. His dark eyes and hair have my pussy clenching with all kinds of wicked wants.

"Yes," I say, bending down to place my lips against his. As if I was ever really anything but his? If I ran where would I go anyway?

Alzerro

I roll over in bed, accidentally moving my shoulder. Fuck. Sharp pain shoots through my arm and deep into the bone. I clench my teeth, holding back the growl that desperately wants to escape my lips. I don't want to wake Bree, though. She's been more than a little concerned with what is going on with my shoulder, and I don't want to stress her out anymore, especially since we're basically in the middle of a war between the mafias.

I look down at her. Her skin has small bruises and scratches on it, and I can't help but run a finger along one of the marks wishing my touch could simply make it disappear.

A soft whimper escapes her beautiful lips, and I feel my dick growing hard. I know that I shouldn't be messing around. I know I need to save my strength, but I survived because of this woman. I had considered her a weakness, but she's the strongest fucking *Piccolo*, even stronger than I.

Sitting up slowly, I move to my knees. She's on her belly, which is fine with me. I slowly wiggle out of my pajama pants. Pulling up the hem of her night shirt, I notice all she has on is a thong. I swallow the lump that forms in my throat. She's sexy as fuck… I imagine how her ass will look rosy red as I smack it repeatedly. Will her skin glow red as I pound into her from behind? Will she purr and moan, begging for more of me?

I pull myself from my thoughts, as I slowly stroke my cock which is sitting at full attention, ready to take her as its next victim. Spreading her legs and pulling the thong back and to the side, I bend down and begin licking deeply. Her ass cheeks move as I nip at her entrance.

"What the…? Ah… Ah…." Her questions turn into moans and pleas for more. She humps my face as I deliver lick after lick. She tastes delicious just as she always does. I pull away, entering her deeply with one finger.

"More… Fuck me," she begs. I smile against her skin. She won't be getting off that easily.

"Ride my hand, baby," I growl, gripping her by the back of the neck. She arches her back, her pace picking up. I watch as her pussy slides over my finger over and over and over again. If I don't stop her, I'm going to come just from watching her.

"Stop," I gently command, releasing her and pulling my finger from her entrance. She whimpers, but only slightly, as I situate her face down, ass up. Her legs are on the outside of mine, and her pussy is saturated with need. That need is for my cock.

She presses back against me as I use my good arm to grab her hip and hold her in place. I smile. My *Piccolo* is very eager for my cock…

"Is that pussy hungry for my cock?" My voice is just on the verge of slipping into animalistic territory. I want her so badly, I'm just not sure what part of me wants her more - the evil side of me that says keep her forever, or the newer side of me that says let her do what she wants. Either way, in this very moment, I know nothing will stop me from fucking her like I own her. She's mine and always will be.

I slam balls deep into her. She clenches around me, holding me in a vice that is so tight, I almost pass out. "Every time I slip inside this tight pussy, it's like heaven—you're like heaven." She makes no attempt at speaking, she merely moans and pushes back against my cock.

I slip out of her and back into her with ease, her tight pussy taking every inch of me. My hand bites into her flesh, and I can't stop myself. Even if my shoulder will hurt later, it will be worth it. I grip her by the back of the neck again, making her fall to her stomach and arch for me.

She whimpers as I hit deeper than I ever have before.

"Who owns this pussy?" I ask between clenched teeth. I have no ownership of her. Not anymore. But I still want to hear her say it. I still want her to say I own her.

Her eyes close, and I grip her neck tighter, plowing into her deeper. My lips are on her ear as I whisper the words again, "Who owns this tight cunt, *Piccolo*?" A shudder runs through her as I plow into her again and again.

"You do. You... Do..." she barely gets out in between breaths. My chest is heaving and my balls are tightening. I want to come so badly, but I know doing so will be the end of our bodies being one, and I can't handle the separation yet. Except, the pleasure is too great, and with one last push to the end of her wall, I come. Her walls clench around me as she cries out, meeting her own orgasm.

Releasing her, I collapse onto her back. I pull myself from her and roll to my side right away, dragging her with me. Her eyes are closed, and her face has this content and blissfully-gone look on it. I smile, knowing it's I who has given her that look. It has only been a day, but I feel closer to her now than I had before. I still haven't opened up about anything, and we haven't talked about what happened, but words aren't needed when bodies can do the communicating.

A sigh comes from her lips as she peers up at me, finally opening her incredible eyes. I'm certain I will never get used to looking at something as beautiful as she. She has taught me that in the blink of an eye, life can end. Without her there yesterday, I would be dead right now. Even though I've killed many people, and I probably deserved to die, I'm alive and am grateful for it. I'm not saying I'm turning over a fucking new leaf because I'm not, but when it comes to her, I will try to be a better man.

"You're such a dirty talker…" she whispers breathlessly. I smile, laying a kiss against her forehead. She has no idea. In that moment, when my cock met her pussy, there was nothing else that I could say. The words I spoke, though dirty, were true.

"Dirty talking is just another thing I'm good at."

Her deep brown eyes roll as if to say shut the fuck up. I know I'm cocky, but when you're me, you have a reason to be.

"We shouldn't have done that. If Jared finds out you were getting rowdy with me, he's going to be pissed." Her concern for me and my safety over Jared has me laughing. She doesn't know Jared like I do. He's a friend, a very close friend, who I met back in grade school before I knew I had responsibilities, before I knew I would be the king of a mafia. That was back when I was normal, when I had a mom and did things that were normal.

"Jared isn't the big, bad wolf, Bree. He's just an old friend who also happens to work for me. He couldn't kick my ass if he tried."

"Oh really, asshole?" I hear Jared's voice on the other side of the door just before he walks in. I pull the covers up over Bree who is still blissfully happy with her post orgasmic face.

"Call me sir, douchebag," I smirk at him. He comes to sit in one of the chairs by the door.

"I called Mack. He said he'll be up in a few days. He wanted to lay low since you caused a complete shit storm. They were raiding every part of your house looking for you and her." My blood boils as I look down at Bree.

They are looking for her and going through all of my things. My personal fucking things! The very things that I've earned, that make me the person I am, are probably destroyed. The fucking nerve of these people! Luccio deserved to die. He was going to kill me, so it was either him or me. When it comes down to a bullet, I will always choose to put one in the other person.

"I didn't cause a shit storm," I proclaim, pulling myself from the bed, and pulling on my sleep pants. Bree is about to doze off again, and I don't want to cause a bunch of fuss.

I get up, and Jared follows behind me, closing the door. We head into the kitchen where I rummage through the fridge for the juice. Once I find it, I pour a glass and take a long drink from it.

"What the hell happened? I thought you were doing the right things? You had me driving you all over the place. That girl in there told me that you found out who killed your mom. When did you start claiming women? What the fuck happened?" Jared rambles, obviously stressed and confused by what is going on.

"Bree was never meant to be anything. She simply fell into my lap. I did what I had to do. I took her in return for a debt that was owed. She was my indebted, now it's I who is in debt to her." I slam back the rest of the juice and wipe my mouth.

"So, she's not yours, but you dragged her into this fucked up, sick, and twisted mess?" The thought of her no longer being mine has my blood boiling. Isn't she still mine?

"Like I expected this shit to be so out of hand? Luccio was my family. Well, kind of. He took me in when I lost everything, but he put the knife in my back. I had no other option but to kill him. Like I told Bree, it's kill or be killed."

Jared runs a hand through his dark hair, looking away from me and up at the ceiling as if he can't believe the shit I've gotten into. It's fucked up, yes, but it's just the start to the war that is on the verge of coming.

"I've known you forever, Zerro. You always told me you had it under control. Now, you have a full on war with another family on your door step and a girl you don't really know if you can trust or not." He eyes me.

"She's a farm girl. She was away at college, Jared. That's cause to say she's dangerous? She was simply paying a debt off that her father owed me," I snarl at him, my grip on the glass in my hand is tense, and I'm afraid that if I don't let it go soon, we will have glass shards all over.

Moving a couple steps forward, he laughs in my face, his expression telling me he doesn't believe a fucking thing I'm saying to him. When did I get off my game so much? When did I start allowing people to act like this?

"Zerro," he says my name as if he wants to say something else, so I stand there waiting for him to spit out whatever he wants to say. "You're right. She's probably innocent, but that's not the point. If she is, then you've dragged her into something that is dark and violent. She won't be able to go back to college for a while, and her life has completely turned the fuck upside down."

"You aren't helping…" I mutter, a feeling of guilt washing over me. I'm never guilty of doing anything. I've killed hundreds of people, but that woman in there has me feeling guilt. Guilt that is going to eat away at me every time I look at her beautiful face.

"I'm not trying to," he retorts. My fist unclenches, releasing the glass onto the marble counter. It falls, breaking into a million pieces. The shards shatter in every direction, but I don't even care as I bring my fist back down onto the counter.

"I won't feel guilty for anything I did, Jared. It had to be done. I've killed countless…." I pause for a moment, looking him straight in the eyes. "Countless people. I've killed for no reason at all. I feel no remorse for any of it."

"But you feel guilty for dragging her into this… Don't you?" His voice is quiet, and I can barely hear him over the blood rushing in my ears. My heart is pumping at Mach speed, or at least it feels like it. Do I feel guilty for it? I've held a gun to her head and wrapped my hand around her delicate neck many times. Neither of those things make me feel guilty, though. Why? *Because you know you'll never kill her.* The thought enters my mind without resistance. Have I always known that I won't kill her?

I can't answer Jared even though I know the answer is deep inside of me. I've dragged someone who is in fact innocent into my shit hole. The very fact that he's right has me growing angrier.

"It's not like I meant for any of this to happen…"

"You feel guilt though, don't you?

I'm avoiding his question. I don't want to admit that I hate what I've pulled Bree into. I don't want to admit that I have feelings for her. At least not aloud. Caring for someone just means another weakness. Caring for my parents has led me to believe that anyone you love will be ripped from you. Caring and loving just puts an X on your back; enemies will know how they can hurt you the most.

"You're such a fucking hard ass…" Jared mutters, shaking his head in disbelief. "Just admit it. For the first time in your fucking life, admit you care about someone."

"Just stop…" My muscles are taut with aggression. I feel the need to kill something or someone right away.

Jared is starting to look really appealing on the ground in a puddle of blood...

"It's not weakness to care for someone, Zerro. I can tell you right now that when I saw you on the ground, I thought the worst. Then there she was, standing there with a gun trembling in her hands ready to take anyone out who even looked at you the wrong way. She's stronger than you give her credit for…"

My heartbeat speeds up as it fills with adoration and something else—love? It can't be. I don't love anyone. Love isn't even a word that I know how to say. Still, she saved my life, so I feel as though I'm indebted to her. Most people would've left me there to fend for myself.

"Fuck. Okay, I feel guilty for putting her in this situation…" My clenched hands unclench as I think about her lifeless body on the ground, a bullet hole in her head, her body surrounded by a dark rimmed puddle of blood. I can't handle it. I can't let her die. Not at my hands. I'm a monster, a sick and sadistic one, but when it comes to her, I feel different. It's no butterflies and sunshine bullshit, but it's something that causes my heart to race and my blood to boil. She's becoming something to me.

"I knew it," he says, smirking at me. I raise my eyes to his. He has a smile on his face. The fucker knows what it takes for me to admit something, and he's rubbing it in my fucking face?

"Get the fuck out of here, before I wipe your face with the floor." I turn on my heels, heading to get the broom.

"I'll remember that at your wedding, asshole." His words stop me in my tracks. Wedding? I hear the front door slam and know he has taken my advice on leaving, although not before leaving me with the thought of marriage. Can I ever get married? Can I commit to someone? Will Bree even be able to handle someone like me?

She's strong, given everything that has happened in the past twenty-four hours, but to have to go through it every day for the rest of her life… Can she do it? The better question is, can I let her?

I walk around the house aimlessly, going stir-crazy. For the first time in my life, I have no answers as to what to do. If the FBI is on my ass, there isn't a lot that can be done. Hiding is all that can get them off your radar for a while. Then the second you fall back into the limelight, they will be on your ass again.

Bree has slept the whole afternoon, and though I want to wake her, every time I walk into the room to do it, I can't. She looks so at peace in the bed that I know if I wake her, the peacefulness that resides within her now will be gone.

Instead, I sit in the chair across from the bed and watch her delicate body. I appreciate her plump lips, the slope of her back, and the way her mouth parts as she allows a sigh to escape her lips as she sleeps.

She's magnificent, and she's mine. No longer able to hold back, I slip back into bed beside her. I need her to wake up. I need to talk to her, tell her how much her life has changed. The moment she saved my life is the moment she became a part of this war.

"*Piccolo…*" I whisper in her ear. She doesn't move, and for a moment I think she doesn't hear me. That is until my eyes sweep across her face. Her big, brown, doe eyes are wide open, peering up at me.

"What time is it?" she asks, her voice full of sleep. I smile at the sound.

"It's late. I just figured after letting you sleep all day you would want to get up." She rolls over, stretching. My dick automatically awakes, rising to the occasion. Of course, the fucker wants to interfere right now when I have business to talk about.

Her eyes roam the room as if she's looking for something. I wonder what she's thinking. Is she scared, worried, afraid? Does she think I will kill her after everything that has happened between us?

"What is going on in that head of yours?" I ask, pushing a lock of hair behind her ear. I've never been the type to caress, touch, love. There isn't a bone in my body that is made for such simple touches.

"I'm just thinking how much things have changed. When I woke up, it took me a second to realize where I was and what was going on."

Sighing, I look deeply into her eyes. "Things are going to change. Whatever life you had before this is gone. You and the person you used to be are gone. The second you saved my life is the second that everything changed for you."

A smile pulls at her lips as her brown eyes sparkle brightly in the light. "My life changed the moment you took me…"

"I know that, but I mean it will never be the same. Ever. Whatever freedoms you had before, you don't have now. I know I promised you that you could leave, and you can. I swear to God, when all this is over if you want to run, you can. You can go wherever the fuck you want to go, but just know that while you're here with me, you're mine." I'm being possessive, and I don't even fucking care. What Jared said to me hit a nerve.

"Yours? I kind of like the sound of that." She laughs softly.

"Yes, mine. Now, I have a plan, and it's going to involve us staying in hiding for a while." I'm never one for running and hiding, and if I didn't have someone I actually care about for the first time in my life beside me, I wouldn't be hiding now either.

"What's your plan?" she asks, genuinely curious about what I'm going to say.

"Mack is coming…" She cringes slightly at the sound of his name, and I'm still wondering why. Did he do something to her?

"Great. What else?" She sounds completely displeased with the idea of Mack, and I can't help but ask her what the problem is.

Moving closer to her, I rest my hand on her shoulder. "Is there something I should know about? Did Mack do something to you?" There have been so many times when I allowed him to go downstairs and check on her without my knowledge of what took place.

How could I be so fucking dumb? She's a beautiful woman, of course he did something. Any man would.

"No…" Bree's voice shakes as the lie escapes her lips. Anger rushes through me as my hand slips from her shoulder and up to the back of her neck where I grip her tightly, pulling her face into mine. Our lips are almost touching when I speak.

"Never. I mean never lie to me. Tell me whatever you have to, but never lie to me. Dishonesty will get you killed faster than anything in this world. Even if it hurts to tell the truth, say it anyway because at least you said it."

My eyes dart over her succulent lips, and the thought of taking her tongue into my mouth is sending my thoughts to all the wrong places.

"Now tell me what he did." I try to hide to need from my voice and the fact that I want to take her against the wall right this second and forget about all the shit in our lives. The problems will still be here when I get done with her, right?

Her eyes gaze down and away from mine as if she's too ashamed to speak. My heart starts beating out of my chest. If she has been with him, I don't know what I will do. Will I kill her right here? Right now? That is the ultimate betrayal.

Her lip quivers, and I swear I see tears swimming in her eyes before she blinks them away.

"He got a little grabby and rough with me. I don't like him and given the chance, I would stab him in the heart. Better yet, I might just shoot him." She sounds vicious and sexy as hell when she's angry.

"When did he touch you?" I ask, withholding my rage. There's no point in showing her my anger. It wasn't her fault. What am I supposed to do, though? I still have to somehow work with Mack. I have to find a way out of this, but he's my main man.

"That night he got me out of the basement, the night you came home with that girl," Bree replies. Fire builds in her eyes when she says that girl. Who did she think I was bringing home? I don't bring women to my private home.

"What did he do to you?" I clench my teeth, not wanting to hear what he did. Her eyes glaze over, and it's as if she's reliving the whole scene. Her body shakes as a single tear escapes her eye. Had I been that dark and uncaring that I hadn't noticed someone who is mine, and mine alone, had been violated?

"He just wouldn't leave me alone. He touched me and pushed me down on the stairs in the basement. He told me I was a distraction for you…" She sounds hurt, as if she wants me to contradict what Mack said. Except he was right: she's nothing but a distraction. She wove herself deep under my skin and somehow made her way into my black heart, causing it to beat again.

"Did he…?" I can't even say it. If he touched her like that, my patience for anything will be gone. I will kill him. I will rip him to shreds, detach his limbs, and feed him his dick.

She shakes her head no, her dark hair cascading into her face. My heartbeat stops, and I suck a breath in between my teeth.

"I'll make him pay… I promise. The second I'm done with needing him, he'll die." I say softly, placing a kiss against her warm skin. In this crazy ass, shit hole, she's the one thing holding me together. Without her here, I would shed more blood. I would be bathing in my enemy's blood.

"Why do we need him?" she squeaks out, my lips still against her skin. I peer down at her.

"He's our ticket out of here…" I mumble.

"Can't we just run?" she asks.

"No. Running is for the weak. We will hide, and when the time is right, I will strike, killing every single one of them." The need for vengeance can be heard in my voice, and I don't even care if it scares Bree. What they have done to me is something that they will pay for.

"So we hide until the time is right and then you kill them all?" she enquires, tipping her head sideways. I release her head and sink back onto the bed.

"The only option is death, Bree. I don't know how many times I have to tell you this, but that's how things are paid for. If they can so easily attempt to kill me, then they should die for trying. It has always worked this way." Frustration fills my body to the brim. How badly I wish I didn't have someone whom I care about!

"You act like I don't get it…" she whispers, getting up from the bed. Does she get it? I'm not sure she understands the danger that she put herself in. Saving me should've been the last thing she ever did. She should've ran when she got the chance.

"Saving me put you here. If you didn't want this, then you should've ran when you had the chance." I don't mean to sound like an asshole, but she has to know what will come from this.

She stops dead in her tracks just inside the bathroom door and turns to face me, her face a pure mask of anger.

"I saved you because it was the right thing to do. I saved you because, even though you're a ruthless killer who has threatened to kill me on more than one occasion, I've grown to want you. I've grown to feel for you. Now, saving your ass by killing that fucker has put an X on my back too."

As her words assault me and her eyes hold a fire so deep that I feel like reaching out and touching it to see if it really will burn me, it hits me. She made the choice; she made the decision. Running wasn't even a thought to her when she pulled the trigger.

I smile smugly. I may be a ruthless killer who is deadly with his hands, but I'm also someone who can bring my *Piccolo* pleasure over and over again. She allows my deadly hands to touch her body. She sees the good in me, even when the bad overpowers it. She accepts me the way I am.

"You saved me even after everything…" I whisper, not really meaning to say it out loud. I know she hears it, though, the minute her eyes darken with lust and she smiles. She's ready for me again, I'm sure. This is dangerous—she's dangerous. Even if I don't want to admit it, she causes my heart to beat harder and faster, and suddenly my thoughts turn to taking her against the wall again.

I keep gazing out the window, pulling back the shades as I wait for Mack to show the fuck up already. He said he would be here soon... Obviously his soon and my soon aren't the same.

"You never told me about your family. Do you have brothers or sisters?" Bree asks, so I turn around to face her. She has on one of my shirts and a cup of tea in her hands. She let me fuck her two more times before saying she needed to shower. Then I climbed in and took her a third time. She's addicting.

"No siblings who I know of. My father and mother are both dead." Saying it always makes it seem real again, which hurts far more than the bullet wound in my shoulder. I never talk about my parents to anyone, so I don't know why I'm spilling my guts to her.

"No siblings for me either. My mom got sick not long after I was born." She sounds defeated as she talks about her mom. I knew when her father came for money what his story was. His wife had died from cancer, so he was alone with a daughter and needed to find a way to make ends meet.

"What type of cancer did she have?" I ask, wanting to take the focus off myself, even if only for a short amount of time. There's a pause as she takes a drink from her cup. Once her lips leave the rim of the coffee cup, she seems to be lost in memories.

"Ovarian cancer." I know nothing about cancer. It has claimed many people in this world, but I've never had taken the time to learn more about any of it, and I've never met anyone with cancer. We don't hang around death. We simply kill and go on our way.

"I'm sorry," I offer sincerely. I'm not sure what else to say. What is someone like me who has more blood on his hands than anyone to say to someone who has lost a parent to cancer? Even worse is that I was going to take her father, her last living relative. I know exactly why she gave herself up. I understand.

"Don't be," she hiccups. A small tear streams down her cheek. Her doe eyes smile at me as her lips shake. What the fuck? Why the hell did I bring this up?

"I am, though," I reiterate, moving closer to her. I may be hateful and so very fucked up, but my heart breaks for Bree. It breaks because I know what it's like to be alone in a world full of people. I know how quiet it is even in a crowded room.

My hands wrap around her, wanting nothing more than to shield her from the pain. How can that even be possible, when I'm the only person in the room who can bring her pain?

"What about your parents?" she asks, smiling. My arms drop from her sides instantly. Can I talk about this with her? Can I tell her how my mother had been killed by the very people who were trained to protect this country?

I feel the coldness seeping into my bones, the walls coming back up. Can I do this to her? Can I make her tell me her secrets without telling her my own?

"I…." I'm stuttering over my words. I'm actually, for the first time in my fucking life, left speechless.

"My mom was killed," I state in such an obvious manner. I know she knows that much, but she doesn't know how it happened.

"I know," she says calmly, as if waiting for me to finish my sentence.

I sigh, taking a step back to sit on the oversized chair. I'm actually going to tell her the story. Memories assault me: the crying, my mom's screams, the fear I felt in her words.

"She was killed when I was eight by the FBI, or at least that's what's being said now... I don't know why, and I don't know who did it. She was a good woman and was never involved with anything that my father had dealt with."

I watch Bree approach the side of the couch slowly before deciding it's safe enough to take a seat next to me.

"I swore from that moment on that I would do whatever I could to find her killers, that I would hunt them down and destroy them… Every member of their family would suffer for her loss. They owed me their lives, and I promised to collect."

My eyes stay trained on the floor. I can't look at her.

"So you planned on avenging your mother's death?" she asks, her voice so soft.

"I didn't just plan on avenging her death. I planned on ripping those people from their loved ones as they took my mother from me. She was the last thing I had when it comes to a family. I was left with no one when she died. I'm the heir to the King money and mafia crown."

A moment of silence passes, and I look up to see if she's still with me.

"Killing people never brought her back, though, and it just ate at you, at your insides. I know it did because looking at who you are now and the person you were when I first met you, seems as if I've met two different people."

I close my eyes. This is the problem. I exhale a deep breath.

"People get used to this side of me without knowing that I can change in a moment's time. I protect myself and that's it. Until—you. I was so keen on getting my revenge through my family's mafia that it never occurred to me what I was doing. I've killed hundreds of people, Bree. There's so much blood on my hands, sometimes it takes me to the darkest places in my mind if I think about it too long."

Setting her glass down on the table, she moves closer to me. Her hands find mine. "Killing people won't bring her back. Doing what you do won't bring her back. Two wrongs don't make a right…"

My eyes pop open as I stare at her face. She feels sorry for me. She sees me as that young boy who lost his mom, who lost everything, and that's not what I want. I don't want pity for what I've done or gone through.

"I don't want your pity, Bree. I don't want you to tell me what I can and can't do, what will work and won't work. We all have our own ways of working through things, and I get by just fine with what I do…" My voice is so full of anger that I have to clench my hands from lashing out at her.

Why does what she says bother me so fucking much? *Because she's right,* my mind whispers to me, which just makes me angrier, of course.

Her mouth parts, and it looks as if she's going to say something. Then she closes it only to open it again. "I don't feel sorry for you. That's the last fucking thing I feel for you. The blood on your hands is because of you, and there isn't any type of pity or saying sorry that can make that shit go away. I just know what it's like to lose a fucking parent, so I feel your pain."

Her words just make me angrier. She knows what pain feels like. Yes, she lost a parent, but she still has one, or at least something similar to one. I have nothing. I have me, myself, and I. Relying on anyone else would just lead to death.

"Pain. You have no fucking clue what pain is…" I sneer. My muscles are clenching with the need to pound on something, and I know the moment Bree notices. She takes a step back, and she's smart to. I'm a ticking time bomb…and she's right in the way of getting hit.

"I do!" she shoots back. She may have backed up away from me, but her face says she could give a fuck about how angry I am. Either way, I've had enough of her defiance.

Standing, I corner her. She thinks I'm evil and dark; she thinks I won't hurt her. She thinks wrong.

"Don't touch me. I don't know you when you're like this…." Her cry is the one thing that causes me to gentle my touch as I grip her by the throat. My nose skims over her skin, settling just over her heartbeat. It's fluttering so fast, I'm afraid it will burst from her neck.

"You know me, as does your body," I whisper, placing a soft kiss against her throat.

"My body wants you, but that's it," she lies. I can tell, I know, she wants me. She wants me for me. The killer in me wants her dead, but the lover in me wants to fuck her senseless. I don't know which one will win.

"You lie…" I growl, nipping at her skin with my teeth. A deep moan escapes her lips. She's the worst fucking liar on the face of the earth.

"I don't," she says with an anger in her eyes that causes my dick to rise. Using my other hand, I slip in between her legs. Evidence of her arousal and need for me is dripping from her leg. She's wet for me.

"The proof is in the pudding, baby..." I growl, slipping a finger inside her. My other hand is still wrapped around her throat. I'm in control, and I want her to know that. We have shared something that I haven't with anyone else, but I don't want her to think she can pull the wool over my eyes. It will always be me who owns her. Me who loves her….

Love? My attack stops as I pull away from her. My hands leave her, and I can tell it upsets her, but I don't care. Do I love her? Love. Why would my mind even think that?

"I thought the proof is in the pudding?" she says slyly, trying to bait me. I lift my face to her, a sinister smile showing. I don't know if I love her, but if my mind tells me I do, then I must. My feelings for her are deep. Love is very possible even if I don't want to admit it out loud.

Dropping my jeans to the ground, I sit back on the couch.

"Ride me," I demand. Her sweet face turns dark as she bites her bottom lip. God, I want to take that fucking lip into my mouth and bite it until I taste blood.

She walks over to me slowly, her hips swaying back and forth. The body of a goddess stands before me.

"Strip… Now…" I say louder than necessary. However, all she does is continue to sway her hips in front of me. My cock is growing harder and harder with every glimpse of her pussy from under my shirt. She wants to kill me. I always thought I would die from a wound, but I'm certain it will be at the hands of this woman.

She giggles as she pulls at the hem of the shirt until it's all the way off. She stands before me in all her glory. She doesn't shy away as I stare at her body. She has seen things most will never understand.

"Fuck me…" I say under my breath as I imagine palming her breast. Her tits are perky, and her nipples are pink.

"At your command, King," she croons softly, stepping forward. My hands instinctively reach out and grip her hips hard. There will be bruises tomorrow, but I don't care. That is just a sign of how intense our love is. Fuck, there's that word again: Love.

"I think I love you…" I whisper against her chest as she sits on my lap, my cock slipping in between us.

"What?" she questions just above a whisper. Her voice is filled with surprise.

"Ride me," I demand instead of repeating what I had just said.

"Wait… Did you say you love me?" she asks. Her eyes are eager to meet mine, and I know she'll know I'm telling her the truth when I look her in the eyes. So I do just that: I look her straight in the eyes.

Bree

Did he just say he loves me? Did Alzerro, the king, actually tell me that he loves me? Is he even capable of love?

"Didn't you just accuse me of lying to you?" I ask. His eyes hold all the answers I will ever need. However, he isn't giving any away. All I can tell is that he meant what he said. He loves me.

"Shut that sassy ass mouth, Bree. Fuck me. Of course I fucking love you. How can I not? You're beautiful. You killed someone for me, and you're still dealing with my ass after all this… So now will you please, pretty fucking please, ride my cock until I'm swelling and my seed leaks out into you?"

Though it isn't the sweetest way to confess your love for someone, it's perfect for Zerro.

"Fuck, yes, I will," I respond, kissing him fiercely.

"That a girl…" he somehow mumbles out while my lips are on his. My hands go into his hair, gripping at the softness of it. He's beautiful, even if he's lost and broken on the inside. I know if I could do anything, it would be to save him from himself.

One of his hands finds its way onto my hip while the other slides in between my legs, honing in on my clit.

He flicks at it softly, causing a swarm of butterflies to escape from my belly.

"Ahhh…"

"You feel that baby? Do you fucking feel that? It's like your soul is soaring as your body takes flight. Your chest fills with air while your mind is going a million miles an hour, but all you can focus on is that one thing that completes you —that's what being with you is like."

Though he's talking, all I can focus on is that one thing—him. All I can focus on is the way his finger flicks back and forth, the way his hot breath feels against my skin, and the way his hand bites into my flesh so painfully that I know he's resisting the urge to slam into me.

"Come for me, baby. Come so hard on my hand, harder than you ever have in your life." At his command, I feel my walls clenching. The delicious feeling of flying zings through me, and I feel as if I'm on the verge of something different - something unseen, something never felt before.

I collapse onto his chest, and just when I think it's over, he slides into me. He places both hands on my hips, holding me in place, waiting for me to come back down from my high.

"You clench me so fucking tightly, baby," he purrs in my ear, his teeth grazing my skin.

Then it's as if I don't just come, it's as if I'm feeling him for the first time deep inside of me. I sit up to look down at him. His eyes are a dark chocolate brown with flecks of gold I had only witnessed once before.

"I'm hungry for you… Starving…" he murmurs, kneading my breasts in a way that has me moving against him.

"I love you," I blurt out, slamming down onto him. I'm working him in and out of me, focusing on my pace, when I think I faintly hear him say, "I know."

I watch as his head tilts back with his mouth open. His eyes are closed, and he looks to be in heaven.

"Fuck yes…" he hisses as I continue to slam down on him. My hips pivot with every movement, and I feel his tip rubbing against my back wall.

"Oh yeah, baby… Ride that cock… Show me who owns you…" His dirty words and seductive voice push me harder.

I stop bouncing and just swivel my hips back and forth. I push down on him hard and am met with a delicious reward. His hands grip my hips harder and harder as he urges me to go harder, my clit rubbing against his cock. Fuck yes. Fuck yes. Fuck yes.

"I… Can't…" I barely get out in between breaths. My chest is constricting, and my body is reeling with pleasurable sparks. His hands slip from my hips and behind his head as I open my eyes and peer down at him. He's watching me ride him with eyes that are glazed over and a soft smile on his lips.

"You can, and you will, come. Again and again, until I tell you that you can't anymore."

"Ahhh…" Is all I can say as I continue to ride him harder and harder. Every slide in and out of him pushes me that much closer to my goal—to the finish line.

"Come. Now!" he yells suddenly. My insides clench around him, and my eyes roll into the back of my head. I stop breathing as beautiful, colorful flashes erupt in my head. I can't stop myself from scratching his chest; my nails dig deep into his skin so deeply, I worry he might be bleeding.

His hands come back up to my hips where he holds me so he can slam into me over and over again. My legs tremble like jelly, and just when I don't think I can take anymore, he's there pushing me to the edge again.

Zerro's cum fills me to the brim as he pushes into me over and over until he grows soft. I fall against his bloody chest, surprised that I did that to him. I can't believe I'm so not myself.

I feel like a bowl full of Jello shivering uncontrollably, so I don't resist him lifting me. My eyes are still closed and my body on fire when I feel the soft blanket covering my body. Sleep invades my body and mind, and I can focus on nothing but the memory of Zerro and his soft smile. I can save him. I just know I can.

I awake sometime later that night, or at least it feels like nighttime. The clock on the night stand says three a.m., but I'm not really sure. My body feels extremely worked over, and I smile shyly, remembering the way Zerro took me before placing me in bed.

I clear the sleep from my eyes when I hear Zerro and another man's voice. I instantly recognize the voice that sends shivers down my spine. It belongs to a face that I would much rather not see. I know all of this before pulling on a shirt and a pair of sleep pants.

"She wasn't ever apart of the plan, Z..." I hear Mack whisper yell. Neither of them know I'm awake yet, and it occurs to me that I can just simply eavesdrop right here.

I hear the sigh that Zerro releases. I can almost see his face; I'm sure it's filled with anger and agony.

"It doesn't matter. She's a part of the plan now, and that's all that matters." My heart swells with love. At least I know he won't be killing me or making me leave him.

"It matters, dude..." I can hear the anxiety in Mack's voice. Something is, very, very wrong.

"Why does it matter? She was nothing before this whole incident and will be nothing after everything takes place. She's clean. I know it." Zerro sounds confident, and though I know I've done nothing wrong, if Mack convinces him that I did do something, I know I'm as good as dead.

"It matters because I know she's not clean. After Jared called me, I did a little digging on her and found some shit out. I never did trust her, and I figured that you should know being that you're the boss."

Horror fills my mind. What is it that Mack could have possibly found out about me that will force Zerro to turn me away or better yet, kill me?

Moments of complete silence pass, and I swear they can hear my heart beating out of my chest. A moment later, Zerro speaks through clenched teeth, "What did you find?" Venom is in every word that leaves his mouth.

"She's the pig. I know it," Mack exclaims proudly. It's as if putting my ass on the line is worth something to him.

"No, she's not. You're so fucked up, Mack. I've trusted you from day one, but accusing someone of such dumb shit is just…" Zerro stops midsentence, interrupted by Mack.

"Really? What's fucked up is that she threw herself at me over and over again. The night I went to get her from the basement is the night that she tried to come onto me. She wanted me to have sex with her and help her escape. She thought that she could use me…" Mack lies.

My eyes grow large at his lie. He's fucking lying to the man I love! He's feeding Zerro lies. They're all lies.

"That's a lie," I declare angrily, walking out of the room. I don't look at Mack whose eyes are probably boring into me; instead, I focus all my attention on Zerro, begging and pleading with him to know the truth, to believe me.

"I told you the truth. I told you what happened," I remind him softly, coming to stand near him. I see the gun in his lap and feel like running for the door.

Mack laughs. He actually laughs. "You honestly want to believe this whore over me? Over one of your most trusted men since you came to leadership?"

"That is such a fucking lie! I can't even stand to look you, much less want to touch you!" I throw at him. I can see the indecision on Zerro's face and that he doesn't know who to believe.

"It's not a lie, and you know it," Mack counters with such force that I can practically feel the hate in his words.

"It is, and if you were half the man you're supposed…"

"Enough!" Zerro screams, causing me to take a step away from him. My body and mind are reeling in an attempt to find the loving man who I had been with only a few hours ago.

"Go stand over there…" He gestures to me, pointing the gun at me. I scurry across the wood floor near Mack, even though it's the last place in the world I want to be.

Zerro's eyes observe both of us. "One of you is lying, and I'm going to fucking find out who." His eyes are black as he swings the gun back and forth between us.

"I've been your right-hand man since before you became the king. You aren't going to accuse me of lying," Mack states.

Zerro cocks his head, an evil look crossing his face. It's then that I know the man standing before me is nothing like the man who made love to me hours before, the man who showed compassion and shared his story with me. Instead, the man standing before me is the shell of that person. This person has no heart, no feelings, and nothing can break him simply because he believes he has nothing to lose.

"Prove to me how you aren't lying."

"How do you want me to do that?" Mack asks, confused. I keep my mouth shut knowing if I talk out of term, my brains could very well be splattered across the wall.

"Tell me this information that you found on her," Zerro sneers, unable to look at me or say my name. That has to mean something, right? That has to mean he feels something for me. That if he points the gun, he won't actually pull the trigger, right?

Mack shuffles his feet back and forth for a moment as if he's nervous. Then he talks, and my life spirals out of control.

"I found out from one of Luccio's men that her father works for the FBI." The second the words leave his mouth, I'm retaliating.

"Lies! It's all lies! This whole thing is a lie!" I frantically assert over and over again. Tears escape my eyes, and I go to turn around, but am stopped. Zerro's hold on me is tight as he places the gun against my lips. His eyes hold no mercy as he bruises me.

"Is that true?" he questions, deathly calm. The tears keep coming, so I'm unable to find my voice to say anything. Without an answer, he loses it.

"Is that fucking true?" he screams, his face right on mine. His hands grip my arms as he shakes me until my teeth rattle in my head.

All I see is a blur of him as I try to get my mind and body to function so I can answer him. My legs hit the floor as he pushes me down, releasing me to walk away. His hand grips his hair as he stares at the gun in his other hand and then back down at me.

"No. No, it's not true," I whimper, tears still falling.

"That's not all, sir." Mack breaks in. What now? What additional lies can he come up with? What more could rip me to pieces than Zerro thinking that my father is in the FBI? That I had betrayed him?

"Tell me," Zerro grits out, his eyes still on mine.

"Don't listen to him," I plead, looking him straight in the eyes.

"Silence," he orders, walking over to me with his hand raised. Will he hit me? Will he hurt me?

"Talk." He turns back to Mack. All I want to do is cover my ears. I don't want to listen to the lies that bastard will spew.

"Not only is her dad in the FBI, but he was the one who shot and killed your mother."

The accusation has me flailing for air. What did he just say? Though nothing about this is funny, I feel like laughing. Mack is crazier than I ever thought.

"That isn't true!" I shoot back. "Nothing he's saying is true…"

Then it's as if Zerro loses it. I feel a hand sweep roughly across my face, knocking me off my knees. I'm unaware of what's taking place because my mind goes blank for a second as my eyes roll to the back of my head. My head throbs, and something trickles down my face, but I can't quite get my wits together to sit up.

"There's more… Her father borrowed the money because he was trying to pin you for something. When it backfired, he sent his daughter in for him. She knew this whole time. She was simply pretending to be something that she wasn't."

"No…" I cry out as my vision swims. Did Zerro hit me? Why does everything I see have black spots in it?

Silence ensues for a long second before Zerro speaks. "Get the ropes and tape!" he yells to Mack. I'm lying on the ground on my side when his face comes into my vision.

"Was it all a lie, Bree? Was it all some fucked up lie, so that you could get into my head? So you could get the inside job done and walk away unscathed?" His voice is so loud in my ears, I push away from him.

"WAS IT?" he demands, his fingers gripping my chin, pulling me closer again.

"No!" I gasp. "I love you! I really and truly do! I don't know what he's talking about. He's a liar!"

I try and push myself up. I need to get up to escape, but I know there's no point in running. Zerro wants me dead. The man I love wants me to die.

"Bind her feet and duct tape her mouth," he orders Mack. Zerro takes a step back, and I await my fate.

"I didn't do it..." I cry and beg. My pleas go unnoticed, though, as Zerro finds a container of something and starts drinking it straight from the bottle.

"Shut up, you stupid bitch," Mack says smugly, pressing my face into the wood floor. More blood falls from my face, and I feel the blackness begging to take me under.

"Listen to me!!!" I demand over and over again. Nothing changes in the way Zerro looks at me. I know the hate he has for the people who killed his mother, and I know that even the absurd possibility of me having any relation to them will do me no good.

"Leave the duct tape off. I want to hear her screams when I shoot her in the head," Zerro coldly commands. His voice is far off, and I wonder if it's me who's slipping away or him.

My body is pulled up until I'm resting on my knees before him. Is he really going to kill me? Is this the end?

I look into the eyes of the man who took me, the man who I had saved from death, but I see nothing of the person I fell in love with. I know today isn't just my funeral, but his as well. With my death will come guilt and heartache like he has never felt before.

The gun in his hand is cocked and loaded. The light glistens off the metal as I watch him raise the barrel toward the side of my head.

"Tell me you didn't know, Bree…" His face is the same of the beautiful man I made love to merely hours ago. Our love is magnificent, but in the big world of things, it's nothing. Fear courses through me as I wait for him to pull the trigger. He'll do it… I've watched him kill too many people to think otherwise. He always pulls the trigger…

"Tell me! Tell me you didn't fucking do it, Bree! Tell me that this bullet isn't for you. Tell me because right now, I'm contemplating killing the one person who means more to me than anything else in the world!" Zerro's voice, though frantic and anguished, is soothing me and giving me hope. Maybe, just maybe, our love can conquer the darkness that is lurking close to his surface.

There's no point in begging him. I know it will do nothing for me, but I have to try to make him understand Mack is lying. "I didn't… I didn't know, I swear...He's lying! My God! How could I've even known you were going to be at my house to collect from my father the day I came home on break? You met my father whom you, yourself, described as weak and simple minded. You honestly think my father could kill someone? He didn't even fight to save me, his own daughter! He let you take me because he was scared of you! There's no way a simple, spineless farmer could be a tough, intelligent FBI agent..." My voice halts in the midst of me trying to convince him I'm telling the truth. Time stands still as Zerro stares into my eyes. He's looking at me, but doesn't see me. Hate and anger come to the surface with a vengeance.

"He's your father, Bree. You had to have known. Payment is due, and this bullet has his name written in your family's blood. So, I suppose this bullet is meant for you." He refuses to listen to reason, refuses to believe me. Gone is the man I've grown to love and care for. I know death is imminent when I feel the cold metal of his gun against my head,

"Any last words?" His voice is so cold that I barely recognize it as the same tender voice that proclaimed his love for me only hours ago.

"You have to believe me! Look at me! Look at me and tell me you can't see that I'm telling the truth. It's Mack who is lying, Zerro! Please. You once claimed you could always tell when I'm lying. Why can't you tell now?" I'm breathless, drowning in my own tears as I try so desperately to make him believe me.

"Why can't I tell now? I'm the king, Bree. From the very beginning, I was taught to trust no one, and that's how I lived my life. Until you...until you came and clouded not only my mind, but my judgment as well. I want to believe you. I really do, but I'm in the middle of a war. Not only with Luccio's people, but with myself. I'm at a fucking, raging battle with myself because of you! The good you unlocked in me is fighting to be free, but the dark, evil, fucked up part of me is telling me not to trust either one of you. That part of me wants to see both of you with bullets in your heads."

Time stands still as I take a deep breath. There's nothing else to say. The monster has been set free, and he won't be at peace until I'm lying on this very floor in a puddle of my own blood.

The silence is literally killing me, it surrounds us, sucking the life right out of me.

"Pull the trigger!" I scream. I feel every single shred of hope leave me. My body, mind, and soul shut down. I'm ready; there's no other way around it.

"I will." Placing his lips against my forehead, he pulls the trigger. He actually pulls the trigger! The sound of the gun going off is loud as Zerro's beautiful face is the last thing I see before my world goes dark.

to be continued

acknowledgements

This is always the hardest part of the book. How does one decide who is better to put at the end of the book when everyone means something to me? First off, I have to give it to my girls - Angela, Tina, Brie, and my street team: you bad bitches are awesome. To my betas: for always being on my ass about feedback. Angela: you seriously do handle stress well. Tina: no more convos about balls burning. Brie: our late night convos are the best. To my marketing gals: you guys rock my socks. I would be making zero money if it weren't for you. Keep shaking those money makers. Bloggers: you guys are awesome. Thank you for all the things you do for me; thank you for reviewing and signing up for shit at the last minute. To all aspiring writers: keep that writing shit going. Someday it will pay off.

J.L. Beck is the Amazon Best Selling Author of the Bittersweet Series. She lives in Elroy, Wisconsin with her husband Brandon and daughter Bella.

Since the moment she could reach the shelves on the bookshelf, she's been reading, thus influencing her to write. Her favorite books are those that leave an imprint on her soul. You know, the ones that have you putting everything off because you have to find out what happens next.

When she's not writing or reading, you can find her picking up after her three year old daughter or explaining to her husband why it's unsafe to do something any other way than the way his wife told him to.

She's a huge fan of all things drama, with shows like *The Vampire Diaries* and *Arrow* being among her favorites. She's addicted to all things social media, caffeine, and Starbucks.

If you feel the need to stalk me, you can find me on:
Twitter: https://twitter.com/AuthorJLBeck
Facebook: https://www.facebook.com/Jo.L.Beck?ref=hl

To keep up to date with all book related stuff please join my newsletter: http://eepurl.com/2aydr

Thank you. XOXO

Made in the USA
Monee, IL
11 December 2021

84810494R00105